He moved closer so they were standing inches apart by the table.

Maddi couldn't look away from his eyes. They were dark, but she could see golden lights very deep. Like fires burning. She was burning inside. She couldn't breathe.

Aristedes lifted her hand and held it close enough to his mouth for her to feel his breath. Her breasts felt heavy, and something completely new and alien coiled and writhed, alive in her lower body. She felt hungry, but it wasn't for food.

His mouth was...sinful. Firm. Sculpted. She desperately wanted him to touch his mouth to her skin.

But he didn't bring her hand to his mouth. He said softly, "How long exactly are you planning on keeping this charade up?"

The heat haze in Maddi's body went cold. "I'm sorry—what did you say?" Maybe she'd misheard him?

He said slowly and distinctly, "We definitely have something we can work with, which would be very convenient if you were, in fact, my fiancée, Princess Laia, but we both know you're not, are you?"

Princess Brides for Royal Brothers

Two forbidden royal matches!

Princess Laia of Isla'Rosa has no intention of marrying the man she has been betrothed to since childhood. She simply needs to avoid walking down the aisle with King Aristedes of Santanger until she is crowned queen. Only then will she have the power to negotiate a different peace strategy between their island nations.

But when the king catches up with Laia, her yet-to-be-announced half sister, Maddi, decides to deflect him—by pretending to be his royal bride-to-be! This sets in motion a series of events that will change the lives of Laia, Aristedes, his brother, Dax, and Maddi in ways they could never imagine!

Don't miss these sumptuous royal stories from *USA TODAY* bestselling author Abby Green:

Mistaken as His Royal Bride

Available now!

and

Claimed by the Crown Prince

Coming next month!

Abby Green

MISTAKEN AS HIS
ROYAL BRIDE

HARLEQUIN

PRESENTS

HARLEQUIN®
PRESENTS™

PLEASE RECYCLE
THIS PRODUCT IS RECYCLABLE

Recycling programs
for this product may
not exist in your area.

ISBN-13: 978-1-335-59305-4

Mistaken as His Royal Bride

Harlequin Enterprises ULC
22 Adelaide St. West, 41st Floor
Toronto, Ontario M5H 4E3, Canada
www.Harlequin.com

Printed in U.S.A.

Irish author **Abby Green** ended a very glamorous career in film and TV—which really consisted of a lot of standing in the rain outside actors' trailers—to pursue her love of romance. After she'd bombarded Harlequin with manuscripts, they kindly accepted one, and an author was born. She lives in Dublin, Ireland, and loves any excuse for distraction. Visit abby-green.com or email abbygreenauthor@gmail.com.

Books by Abby Green

Harlequin Presents

Bound by Her Shocking Secret
A Ring for the Spaniard's Revenge
His Housekeeper's Twin Baby Confession

Hot Summer Nights with a Billionaire

The Flaw in His Red-Hot Revenge

Jet-Set Billionaires

Their One-Night Rio Reunion

Passionately Ever After...

The Kiss She Claimed from the Greek

Visit the Author Profile page
at Harlequin.com for more titles.

This is my sixtieth story for Harlequin. I never dreamed, when I first picked up a Harlequin novel in my grandmother's house in the 1980s, that I would one day be writing for the iconic publisher. It is literally a dream come true. I couldn't have done this without the patience, love and cheerleading of my friends and family. I couldn't have done it without the expertise of my editors. And most especially, I couldn't have done it without the readers. You are the ones who make this job worthwhile.

Thank you!

This is for my mother.

CHAPTER ONE

IT WAS LIKE a scene from a futuristic movie. They were in the middle of the desert under a scorching sun and around them were all manner of eye-popping spectacles.

On a huge stage in the far distance a world-renowned band was blasting out their hits to an ecstatic crowd. There were food and drinks stalls selling everything from healthy smoothies to tequila shots to burgers and Asian street food.

Otherworldly giant figures appeared through the heat haze—people on stilts. At that moment a couple walked past Maddi Smith, hand in hand, and she only realised belatedly that they were entirely naked except for body paint.

There was a circus ground nearby, and Maddi watched a trapeze artist in a sequined leotard with a mane of long bright red hair fly through the air against the bright blue sky like an exotic bird. She held her breath and let it out again when the trapeze artist was safely caught by the hands of her partner.

Huge temporary art installations made of wood—intricate houses, windmills, even ships—were silhouetted against the sky. A man drove across the desert in the distance on a fish-shaped motorbike.

The crowd around them were an eclectic mix of young and old, but with a common theme of eccentricity, a zest for life and wearing costumes that bared acres of flesh and wouldn't look out of place on the cover of a steam punk novel.

'This place is wild, Mads. How on earth did you hear about it?'

Maddi's half-sister Laia put her arm through hers. Maddi's heart swelled. She loved her so much, even though they'd only met for the first time a year ago.

And right now the two half-sisters fitted right into the crowd around them milling through the teepee tent village where they'd slept the night before. Laia was wearing a black diamante bra-top and tiny shorts, fishnet tights and sturdy black boots. Her hair was backcombed and threaded through with tiny plaits. They'd had their eyes painted with sparkles and glitter and bright green eyeshadow.

Maddi was wearing something very similar, but instead of shorts she was wearing a tiny gold mini skirt. They both had huge goggles on their heads, part of their costumes but also protection against the sun and sand.

Maddi squeezed Laia's arm. 'I heard about this place when I was working at the club in Dublin. It's been on my bucket list ever since.'

Laia smiled. 'Is that the place where you had to dress like a French maid?'

Maddi shuddered. 'Don't remind me. I could have worn that uniform here and not looked remotely out of place.'

Laia laughed.

At that moment a man walked past wearing nothing but a thong and a large rug around his shoulders. His sunglasses had a third lens to cover his third eye.

He looked at them and tipped an imaginary hat. 'Ladies.'

The sisters giggled and then Maddi took Laia's hand. 'Come on, let's find some food. I'm starving.'

Laia responded dryly, 'When *aren't* you hungry?'

Maddi made a face at her and led her through the crowd, conscious of the ever-present security detail that accompanied them at a distance. Because Maddi's sister was someone important. Very important. She was Crown Princess of a small kingdom in the Mediterranean called Isla'Rosa. She was due to turn twenty-five in mere weeks and then she would be crowned Queen.

Maddi was the product of an illicit affair Laia's father the King had had about a year after his beloved wife had died while giving birth to Laia.

When Maddi's mother had fallen pregnant the King had panicked and sent her into exile, with an allowance to bring up his illegitimate daughter and an edict to stay away from Isla'Rosa for fear of causing a scandal.

Her mother was a proud woman and had left, taking her broken heart and her pregnancy with her. One of Maddi's abiding memories from growing up was her mother's bone-deep sadness. Her mother had never hidden the origins of her birth, and Maddi had always felt in some part responsible for her pain. If Maddi hadn't been born then they wouldn't be living in exile. Her mother would still be in the country she loved.

Laia had explained to Maddi that she'd only found

out about her when her father had been on his deathbed, racked with guilt and remorse, nearly four years ago.

He'd confessed to Laia that he'd had the affair because he'd been grief-stricken and overwhelmed by becoming a widower with a young baby daughter. It was no excuse, he'd said, but it had been a moment of weakness that he'd always regretted. He'd begged Laia to look for Maddi to try and explain and ask for forgiveness for his behaviour.

But Laia hadn't gone looking for Maddi straight away. She'd been fearful of what she might find. Afraid that Maddi would hate her for being ostracised, and possibly not want anything to do with her. Maybe even be bitter and want to lay her own claim to the throne or harm Isla'Rosa.

But eventually Laia *had* gone looking for Maddi and had found her in Ireland, and from the moment the half-sisters had met, all of Laia's concerns had dropped away. There had been a powerful connection between them. An instant bond. As if they'd already known each other on some level.

When Laia had found Maddi she'd explained that she fully intended to reveal Maddi as her half-sister, and a true Princess of Isla'Rosa—but they agreed it wouldn't happen until the coronation, when Laia would announce Maddi as Princess, once she was Queen.

Their father the King had been much revered by the people of Isla'Rosa and the world over, especially for his lifelong devotion to his deceased wife, so news of an illegitimate daughter and a lover would come as a huge shock—not just to the people of Isla'Rosa.

Maddi didn't want to be the cause of any adverse

headlines before the coronation and she'd made it very clear that she had no designs on Isla'Rosa. The most important thing for her was to get to know her sister. She'd never expected Laia to come looking for her. And she'd had no intention of seeking her sister out, even though she'd known where she was. That whole existence…a royal life of duty and privilege…was so far removed from Maddi's very ordinary upbringing as to be on another planet.

She harboured no bitterness or resentment at having lived a parallel life. She was inherently shy and not academic. In the infrequent moments when curiosity had driven her to look her sister up online, and she'd seen Laia's poise and confidence in social situations, she'd always felt totally intimidated and relieved not to be in that position.

Her sister spoke five languages fluently!

Maddi spoke one.

So in fact she still felt very ambiguous about taking up her rightful place as a Princess of Isla'Rosa. The prospect was terrifying, and she wasn't remotely ready, even though she'd spent the last year working as Laia's lady-in-waiting. It had been Maddi's suggestion when Laia had said she wanted her to return to Isla'Rosa with her.

Working for Princess Laia as one of her staff had afforded Maddi the chance to get to know her sister undercover, and also to get to know her ancestral home.

The last year had been a revelation.

She hadn't expected to fall in love with the small island and its rocky landscape dotted with flowers, its pristine beaches and charming medieval main town,

Sant'Rosa. Or the smiling, friendly people she'd immediately felt connected to.

She hadn't expected to feel as if she belonged somewhere for the first time in her life.

She hadn't expected to fall in love with her half-sister, older by nearly two years. She wasn't just a sister—she'd become a best friend.

For most of Maddi's life she'd kept people at arm's length, aware of the huge secret she carried within her. Aware of the fact that her father had chosen to reject her before he'd even met her. She'd carried it like a bruise all her life, on top of the guilt and responsibility she felt for her mother's exile.

Meeting Laia and going to Isla'Rosa had gone some way to soothing some of those very complex emotions. Maddi even hoped that her mother and Irish stepfather might return to Isla'Rosa for an extended period. But as yet her mother hadn't decided what to do...

As they stood in the queue for food, Maddi smiled at Laia's obvious enjoyment of the spectacle around them. She'd noticed in Laia a growing preoccupation recently as the coronation drew closer, and had suggested this trip as a diversion.

She'd said, 'It'll take your mind off things, and it'll also help maintain your image of feckless socialite with nothing on her mind but fun, even in the face of huge responsibility.'

Laia had looked at her and then stood up from behind her desk in her office at the castle on Isla'Rosa and said, 'Brilliant. Two birds with one stone. When do we leave?'

Maddi felt a prick of guilt that the burden of becom-

ing Queen was all on Laia's shoulders and always had
been, even though it was totally irrational for her to
feel guilty—she'd never been recognised publicly as a
member of the royal family.

And, as much as becoming a princess terrified her,
she knew deep down that it was her destiny now, and
she owed it to Laia and her own mother to at least do
her best to fulfil it. At least then her mother's exile and
heartbreak might not have been completely in vain...

At that moment Maddi noticed the sun glinting off
something in the distance. It was a small sleek plane—
a private jet—touching down on the runway. For some
inexplicable reason a tiny shiver went down her spine.
A sense of foreboding.

She kept looking back, and now she saw the tiny dot
of what had to be a motor vehicle coming towards the
festival, a plume of dust and sand in its wake.

'What is it?' Laia asked. 'What are you looking at?'

'A plane has just landed—a small one. Someone is
coming.'

'People are arriving all the time.'

Maddi couldn't explain why *this* arrival felt different. But now Laia was watching too, and as the vehicle
got closer they could see that it was a black SUV with
tinted windows. It looked official in some way. Offi-
cious. The opposite of the crowd and vibe around them.

Laia tensed beside her and said, almost to herself,
'He wouldn't have followed me here... I mean, I wanted
him to see the pictures we leaked to the press, but to
actually come all this way...'

Maddi knew who she was talking about. The man
who had been growing more and more frustrated by

Laia's reluctance to meet with him, to discuss the fact that they were due to be married. She'd been promised to him in marriage since her birth. An archaic arrangement that had shocked Maddi when she'd first heard of it.

'He' was King Aristedes de Valle y Montero of Santanger, the neighbouring kingdom to Isla'Rosa. Their marriage was to be a union to unite the two kingdoms, which were enjoying a rare period of harmony after hundreds of years of bitter enmity and war.

The only problem was that Laia did not *want* to marry King Aristedes, because doing so would endanger Isla'Rosa's independence. As the smaller country, it would naturally be dominated by the bigger, richer entity of Santanger.

Laia had a vision for Isla'Rosa. She wanted to solidify peace between the countries *not* through an archaic marriage pact but through modern diplomacy, agreements and trade deals. And she was afraid that King Aristedes—known for being a stickler for tradition and rules—wouldn't listen to reason. That he would insist on the marriage and force her into it by appealing to her sense of duty and responsibility.

Laia was passionate about her country retaining its independence, and since she'd come to know and love it so was Maddi.

The car drew to a halt on the edge of the crowd and as Maddi watched, the driver got out and opened a back door. She held her breath. A man uncoiled his tall body from the back of the car, and she knew from Laia's indrawn breath that it was indeed King Aristedes.

Maddi had never seen him in the flesh. Even though

he was still at some distance she could see that he stood head and shoulders over most of the crowd. He was wearing a dark three-piece suit which made him stand out even more among the outlandish costumes. He started to walk through the crowd with a couple of men who had to be his security detail, also dressed in suits and wearing sunglasses.

If Maddi hadn't been as tense as her sister, she might have giggled at how out of place they looked.

Laia's fingers were digging into Maddi's arm painfully. 'I can't believe he came all the way here,' she said.

'You've been dodging meetings with him for months now,' Maddi pointed out. 'We left Manhattan the morning he arrived to try and take you for lunch.'

That had been one among many other similar occasions. Maddi could understand that he must be frustrated. He'd made no secret of the fact that he was ready to wed his convenient bride and have his Queen by his side.

Beside her, Laia said, 'I only have to hold out another couple of weeks, until my twenty-fifth birthday, then I'll be crowned Queen and I'll have much more power to renegotiate the marriage agreement and encourage him to think of other solutions.'

King Aristedes was tracking closer. Moving swiftly through the crowd. Maddi couldn't help but notice how he moved with loose-limbed grace. He was even taller than she'd thought. Shoulders broad, chest wide. He oozed such power and masculinity that the people in the crowd around him noticed and stopped to watch. Which, considering the other eye-popping spectacles around them, was no small thing.

Not just imposing and charismatic, he was also gorgeous, with short dark hair and a strong-boned face. A trim dark beard hugged his jaw. Maddi couldn't see his mouth from here, but she'd seen it in photos. Well-defined. Sensual. Firm. *Sexy.* His eyes were covered now, but they'd appeared dark in the photos.

Maddi realised at that very inopportune moment that she was way more transfixed by King Aristedes than she should be.

She tore her eyes off the man coming towards them and turned to her sister, who was pale. Maddi gripped her arm, 'Laia, look at me…are you okay?'

Laia's gaze went to her sister. She shook her head. 'I feel sick. I can't believe he's still determined to marry me, even after everything I've done to put him off.'

Laia was referring to her well-documented campaign of appearing in public at every glittering party and social event with the sole reason of deterring the famously conservative and staid King Aristedes from pursuing their marriage by making herself look like a party girl.

Maddi said, 'Look, is it really that hopeless? What if you use this opportunity to talk to him and make him see your side?'

But Laia shook her head. 'I tried to talk to him after my father's funeral, but he wouldn't listen. He said very clearly that our marriage would happen the way it had been agreed and he would not discuss the matter further. He showed no interest in who I was. He sees me only as a means to an end.'

'Won't you be risking the peace if you're crowned before the marriage takes place?'

Laia shook her head. 'No, he wouldn't want to look

petty. *We* know the marriage is due to take place before the coronation but it's not common knowledge among the greater public, yet. The itinerary was going to be revealed much closer to the day to minimise the risk, albeit small, of old rebel elements from both kingdoms stirring things up. I can use that to my advantage now. Santanger prides itself on being a modern, forward-looking country, which makes it so ironic that he's intent on this marriage. He'll see it as an inconvenience that things haven't gone exactly to plan, but if he thinks the marriage is still in play he won't care too much. That'll give me the time I need to go to him as an equal head of state.'

Passion mixed with panic made Laia's eyes wide and very green.

'Mads, I don't want to let Isla'Rosa be swallowed up by Santanger. We've fought for our independence in so many battles! Our father set up the marriage agreement under pressure from King Aristedes's father, who engineered it so that the marriage would take place before I turned twenty-five—before I could be crowned Queen—ensuring Santanger maximum leverage over Isla'Rosa.'

She shook her head.

'I think Father thought it would be for my benefit, having my husband by my side before I was crowned Queen but over the years he saw how capable I was and I think he regretted bowing to the pressure. He told me on his deathbed that he didn't want me to marry for anything less than love, no matter how high the stakes, so maybe he was preparing me to rebel against it, if I wanted to.'

She continued, 'He wanted me—*us*—to be happy.
I know I can persuade King Aristedes that a marriage
is not necessary to create lasting peace between us,
but I need to be Queen before I'll have the power to do
that. Until I'm crowned I'm still vulnerable, and King
Aristedes knows that—which is why he's so hell-bent
on pursuing this marriage as soon as possible. It shows
he hasn't changed his view on how this should happen.
He still wants his marriage of convenience and to have
power over Isla'Rosa.'

Love and loyalty swelled in Maddi's chest for her
sister. She knew this was her chance to do something
really useful.

She took Laia's hands in hers and said quickly,
'When was the last time you met King Aristedes face
to face?'

Laia frowned. 'A few weeks after my—' She corrected herself. '*Our* father's funeral, when I tried to talk
to him about the marriage agreement and he refused to
listen. I haven't seen him in years.'

Maddi hid her pang of pain at the reminder that she'd
never met her father behind a wry smile. 'Wow, you've
really turned avoiding him into a sport.'

Laia shrugged and smiled back weakly. 'I did what
I had to, to avoid the inevitable.' She looked over
Maddi's shoulder and gulped. 'But it didn't work. He's
getting closer.'

The back of Maddi's neck prickled, as if she could
feel his presence. Strange... She'd never met the man.
But she was about to.

She squeezed Laia's hands. 'You need to go—*now*.
Into the crowd. Get lost.'

Laia frowned more. 'But...what do you mean? You're coming with me.'

Maddi shook her head. 'No, I'm going to take care of this. You just need to disappear till your birthday, right?'

Laia nodded.

'Then I will make sure King Aristedes is distracted until it's too late.'

'How?'

Maddi smiled even as her insides knotted with apprehension. 'What was apparent the first time we met? How much we look alike. We could pass for twins.'

Maddi had heard the castle staff whispering about the likeness between her and Laia, but no one had had the nerve to speak of it directly.

Understanding dawned in Laia's eyes, but she shook her head. 'No, Mads. I can't let you do something like this. It's too crazy...'

But Maddi was firm. 'You've borne the weight of massive responsibility all your life. Let me do something for you and our country.' Before she lost her nerve she gestured to their bodyguard, who came over. She said, quickly and quietly, 'You need to take Princess Laia away from here. There's a serious security threat.'

He needed no more instruction. He bundled Laia in front of him and they were soon lost in the crowd.

Maddi couldn't believe what she'd just done, but she didn't regret it. She and Laia *could* almost pass for twins. Apart from their eyes. Laia's were green and Maddi's were hazel.

They both had long, wavy dark brown hair. Olive-toned skin. Wide, almond-shaped eyes. Straight noses.

The same mouths. Except Maddi's had a more rosebud shape. And she had a small gap in her front teeth.

They were of similar height, and the only other real difference was one that Maddi lamented, she was curvier than Laia, whose figure ran to being more athletic.

Maddi took a deep breath and turned around. King Aristedes was even closer now, his head swivelling back and forth, tracking everyone in the crowd. She drew her shoulders up straight and looked at him.

As if sensing her gaze, King Aristedes stopped and his head turned towards her. He went very still. Like an animal scenting its prey. The tumult of the crowd around them died away.

He lifted his sunglasses from his face. Maddi's heart thumped. His eyes were deep-set and unfathomably dark. Impossible to read. His jaw was clenched. He moved towards her.

King Aristedes stopped in front of her and she had to tip her head back to look up. He looked at her for a long moment and said nothing, his dark gaze roving over her face and body.

Maddi's skin prickled all over and her insides turned to liquid. Maybe she'd overestimated just how similar she was to her sister. But then King Aristedes spoke. His voice was deep and it resonated all the way inside her.

'The elusive Princess Laia. I think it's time for you to come home and fulfil your obligations, don't you?'

CHAPTER TWO

MADDI WATCHED AS the festival below them in the desert became a smaller and smaller dot. Laia was down there somewhere, watching this plane leave. Maddi sent her a wish that she would escape somewhere until it was safe for her to emerge and become Queen.

She was aware of King Aristedes on the other side of the aisle. She could feel his gaze on her but she was avoiding looking at him. It was like looking at the sun. Too dangerous.

She felt very self-conscious in her costume, which, out of context looked cheap and tacky and bared far too much flesh.

'What on earth was that spectacle?'

Maddi bristled at his scathing tone. Reluctantly she looked at him. 'It's a famous festival. It brings art and music and people together in an extravaganza of creativity and innovation. There's nothing else like it in the world.'

'It looked ridiculous.'

Maddi turned her body to face him and opened her mouth, but then she saw his gaze drop to her chest for a split second. A zing of electricity skated over her skin and it shocked her so much that she forgot what she was going to say.

He raised a brow. 'I think you can remove your… glasses now.'

Maddi frowned, and then realised he was referring to the goggles on her head. She pulled them off, wincing a little as they caught on her hair.

The air inside the private jet suddenly felt cold, and it wasn't just the chilly atmosphere caused by King Aristedes. Air-conditioning. She shivered and he noticed.

He frowned. 'You're wearing next to nothing. Do you have other clothes with you?'

He and his security team had allowed her to go to their tent and collect her bag and other things. So she did have a change of clothes with her. She wasn't sure it was going to be much of an improvement, though. But she jumped at the chance to get out of his disturbing presence even for a few minutes and collect her thoughts.

'Yes, I do. I'll go and change.'

'There's a bedroom and bathroom at the back.'

Maddi stood up with as much grace as she could muster, considering she looked like an extra from a Mad Max movie, and went to the back of the plane.

She closed the door to the bedroom suite behind her and took a deep, shaky breath. She'd done it. She'd fooled King Aristedes into thinking she was Laia. Even if it only allowed Laia enough time to get away it would be worth it.

Maddi looked around the suite. It was sumptuous, but understated, in a palette of cream and gold and beige like the rest of the plane. There was luxurious carpet underfoot.

She'd grown used to luxury since living in the castle on Isla'Rosa, but this was another level.

She put her bag down on the bed and opened it, choosing some clothes to change into.

She went into the bathroom, and the sight of the massive walk-in shower made her very conscious of the thick layer of grime and dust she'd acquired over the last twenty-four hours.

Stripping off, Maddi turned on the water and stepped under the hot steaming spray with a little groan of satisfaction. It took her an age to do her hair and scrub at her face until she was sure all the make-up was off.

When she stepped out, she wrapped her hair in a towel and pulled on a robe. She looked at herself in the mirror and balked—because suddenly the difference between her and her sister looked much starker. She would never get away with convincing the King that she was Laia now.

She was much paler than Laia, having grown up in Ireland, so she hadn't cultivated the natural tan her sister had. Her hair was also a bit darker because she hadn't grown up in the sun. Her eyes looked much darker now, too.

This had been a nuts idea. But it was too late to turn back. And if it allowed Laia to get away to somewhere she could hide out then it had to be worth it.

Maddi got dressed, dried her hair, and then, fully prepared for the King to realise instantly that she wasn't Laia, went out to meet her fate.

* * *

Ari heard the door open behind him and didn't like the way a sizzle of anticipation skated along his nerve-endings. It was most unwelcome. But from the moment he'd locked eyes with Princess Laia in that godforsaken circus amusement park something in his awareness of her had shifted. As if a gear had clicked into place.

She'd never had that effect on him before. Granted, he hadn't seen her in almost four years, and perhaps now that she was a fully grown woman...

'Sorry, I took a shower. I hope that's okay.'

He could smell her before he saw her. Musk and rose. She came alongside him and he turned his head. His eyeline was at her slim waist. She was now wearing short cut-off shorts covered in sequins. Bare, shapely legs led down to a pair of pretty feet in gladiator sandals. Nails painted a coral colour.

His gaze tracked back up and he saw that she was wearing what looked like a lurid pink Spandex leotard under the shorts. No bra. Nothing to disguise the most beautifully shaped breasts he'd ever seen. Full and teardrop-shaped. Nipples hard and pushing against the material.

In an instant Ari was engulfed in more than heat. It was white-hot lust—for a woman he'd been promised to in marriage since she was a baby. And who he'd never had this reaction to before.

Her face was clean now. Paler than he remembered. But still beautiful. She'd grown into her beauty since he'd seen her last.

Those distinctive almond-shaped eyes... He'd always had the impression they were green in colour, but here on the plane they looked darker, almost more golden than green.

And her mouth… Had it always been that provocative, with a naturally pouting bow shape?

His conscience pricked. Did he not even recognise his own fiancée? He doused the heat in his body with ice and said sharply, 'Don't you have something to cover up with?'

Laia sat down in the chair and the movement made her breasts sway under the thin material. Ari could not understand this horny schoolboy reaction to a woman when he'd never indulged in such behaviour even when he had been a schoolboy. Control had always been key and he'd never lost it.

But her body was like a siren call.

He shook off his jacket and handed it over. 'Here, put this on.'

He watched as the Princess slid her arms into his jacket and pulled it over her chest. He immediately lamented her hiding her body from view even as he welcomed it.

Was his reaction due to sexual frustration? Possibly. He'd let his last mistress go a few months ago, to focus exclusively on tracking down his wayward fiancée and making her his Queen. His last few lovers had been disappointing—not just sexually, but on every level—and he'd actually relished not having to play that game for the last few months.

It had galvanised him to follow through on this royal pact. He was ready to settle down. He was resigned to the fact that he would soon be committing to one woman, no matter their compatibility, because he'd vowed that he would never be unfaithful to her.

His father had been serially unfaithful to Ari's mother and it had broken her. Turned her into someone unstable and bitter. Love was for fools. And so was chemistry. It didn't last.

He knew he would like Laia enough to bed her, even if she wasn't his usual type. So this unexpected *heat* he felt was…surprising. A distraction. Princess Laia Sant'Roman of Isla'Rosa had never so much as caused a blip of awareness in him. Another reason why she was so perfect.

What the hell was going on now?

'I can't believe you came all the way to the festival to find me.'

Maddi was still trembling from the excoriating look King Aristedes had just given her. It was clear that he couldn't be more disgusted by her. She cursed herself again for not taking more care to pack her clothes in the tent. For not at least grabbing a sweatshirt or jacket.

King Aristedes's jacket was warm around her shoulders. His scent was tantalising, deep and complex. Tones of leather and wood and something more exotic. She imagined a dark flower, blooming in the rocks against the odds, sending out a musky scent…

King Aristedes said, 'I was growing tired of having my invitations ignored or rescinded. Enough is enough. We have a pact to honour, and it's time to get on with our lives as King and Queen of Santanger.'

Maddi felt a spurt of loyalty to Laia. 'And of Isla'Rosa.

You'd be King of our—' She corrected herself quickly. '*My* country too.'

He inclined his head. 'That is part of the agreement, yes.'

Maddi's hands curled into fists. 'I don't want Isla'Rosa to get lost in this agreement. The pact doesn't say that we have to lose our independence—and yet that is what will happen, isn't it?'

He said with casual arrogance, 'Your marriage to me can only benefit Isla'Rosa, it needs investment to reach its full potential.' And then, 'There's no reason why the privy council who are ruling until you come of age or marry can't go on doing their very fine work. Let's face it: they've proved their ability to rule during your…frequent absences.'

Maddi went cold. Laia had been right. He had no interest in her or her desire to be ruler of her own kingdom. Maddi knew that the members of the privy council appeared to be the ones with all the power, and in many ways they were. But Laia had been assuming more and more control since their father had died, and the council now deferred to her on almost every decision. She was no mere figurehead.

But of course King Aristedes didn't know that, because her sister had been promoting an image of pleasure-seeking sybaritic socialite at every opportunity, in the hope of putting him off.

It was common knowledge that King Aristedes was famously serious and strait-laced. Unlike his playboy younger brother, Crown Prince Dax, who seemed to be his opposite in every regard.

Thinking of the King's intransigence, Maddi said, 'Are you sure this is a good idea? We're not very alike.'

One of Laia's complaints was that she wasn't even his type. He seemed to favour tall, leggy blondes. Ice-cold and perfect. Laia and Maddi bore the features and colouring of their mixed ancestry—Roman, Greek and Moorish.

King Aristedes's deep voice pulled Maddi back to the conversation.

'It's not about whether we're compatible—it's bigger than that. Our marriage will honour a peace pact made by our fathers to ensure long-standing harmony in the region.'

The father Maddi had never met.

It was as if King Aristedes was pushing against that wound, bringing it back to life.

Hadn't her father ever wondered about her? Cared what had happened to her?

Loved her at all?

In a bid to stop her mind going to dark places, Maddi focused on the conversation at hand, while trying not to let herself notice how King Aristedes's muscles moved and bunched under his shirt and waistcoat. She'd somehow imagined the King to be…softer. But this man was the opposite of soft. He resembled a prize fighter in civilised clothing.

'So you have no objection to a marriage that is not built on common interests or love?' she asked.

'None. And nor should you. This marriage is an important strategic alliance. Maybe if our countries had done this a long time ago we wouldn't have suffered so much war and hardship.'

Maddi had studied the history of Isla'Rosa, and by extension some of the history of Santanger, and from those early battles in the Middle Ages right up to the last battle in the last century, it had been brutal.

Maddi still found it hard to get her head around the thought of such carnage on the pretty streets of Isla'Rosa's main town and in the clear blue-green seas around the island. Maybe King Aristedes was right.

Maddi immediately felt disloyal to her sister.

It wasn't that Laia didn't want to do her duty—she did, passionately—but she'd revealed that she wanted to do it with someone by her side who could offer a real relationship. Love and respect and loyalty to the crown of Isla'Rosa, as well as her, of course.

Maddi admired Laia for her idealism about love, but she couldn't understand it personally because she had grown up watching her mother do her best to hide her broken heart. She'd married eventually, and she was now relatively happy, but Maddi had always been aware of the deep sadness inside her.

So Maddi couldn't envisage what it was to strive for love. As far as she could see it just brought pain and destruction. It was somewhat disturbing to realise that King Aristedes was making some sense to her...

'Where are we going?' she suddenly thought to ask, belatedly.

'Straight to Santanger. The wedding will take place in a couple of weeks and there will be a lot of preparation.'

Maddi gulped. Further confirmation that King Aristedes was clearly set on having their marriage take place exactly as planned. No deviation.

A small rogue inside her was tempting her to test him. She said, 'What if we delay the wedding until after I'm crowned Queen of Isla'Rosa?'

King Aristedes looked at her. Stern. No emotion. No softness. 'That is impossible.'

'Nothing is impossible,' Maddi said, hoping to sound defiant but fearing she sounded hesitant.

He shook his head. 'This will happen as per the agreement. You'll become Queen of Isla'Rosa when we marry.'

Yes, but not before you become King of Isla'Rosa through that marriage and its precious independence is gone for ever.

King Aristedes looked impatient. 'You've always known this was the agreement. You've had your whole life to prepare for this moment.'

That was true. She had to be careful. She was responding as Maddi, not Laia. Laia would be cool, calm and collected.

'You're right. I have.'

'And I can trust that you won't do a disappearing act once we land?'

Maddi envisaged Laia on another flight, hopefully to the other side of the world. No way would she jeopardise that.

She forced a smile. 'Of course not. I'm committed to this.'

Right up until he realises I'm not Princess Laia and kicks me off Santanger.

Or, worse, locks her in a dungeon. She wouldn't put it past this brooding taciturn king who had obviously reached the end of his patience to do something so drastic. Laia had shown her the terrifying dungeons in the castle on Isla'Rosa. They'd given Maddi nightmares for weeks.

Clearly satisfied that he had his errant fiancée under some kind of control at last, the King turned back to his laptop.

Maddi could understand Laia's misgivings now. She could see how her sister had clashed with King Aristedes and his arrogance, and had taken the drastic actions she had to try and deter him. But he was like a rock. Immovable.

As for Maddi…she could only imagine what his reaction might be when he discovered the truth about who she was.

'Are you sure you've nothing more substantial to change into?'

Maddi had an absurd urge to giggle at the look of distaste on the King's face. Well, it was an urge either to giggle or melt in a puddle. Because when he looked at her like that he caused all sorts of illicit flutterings deep in her belly.

She glanced down at her attire. The hot pink Spandex leotard and cut-off shorts sparkling with plastic diamonds. Bare legs. Flat sandals. That little rogue inside her was almost glad on Laia's behalf that she was causing such a spectacle.

'I really don't have anything else. It's this…or what I was wearing before.'

They were due to land in the next few minutes.

King Aristedes made a sound and said ominously, 'That will be rectified as soon as we get to the palace.'

Maddi looked out of the window and her heart quickened at the sight of Santanger in the distance. It was officially winter time now, but the sun glinted off the sea and the rocky island as if it was summer. Maddi knew the temperature would still be comfortable. Like Isla'Rosa, it had the perfect all-year-round climate.

A big change from growing up in damp Ireland, where you were lucky to get a summer and rain was a far too frequent reality.

Isla'Rosa was somewhere in the distance, to the west of Santanger. Too far away to be visible. It took an hour to fly from Isla'Rosa to Santanger. As Maddi had heard Laia say under her breath more than once, *'Too close for comfort.'*

As the plane grew closer and closer, Maddi could see a very impressive palace high on a hill overlooking the city down below. The palace made the castle on Isla'Rosa look like a shed. It was seriously impressive, both as an obviously defensive fortress but also as a royal palace, with whimsical towers and turrets.

Waves crashed against jagged rocks and Maddi shivered involuntarily again. She spotted some pristine beaches in the distance. White sands.

They were approaching the airport now, and the runway spread before them, a long black ribbon. The airport building was surprisingly modern. Perhaps an example of progress on Santanger, the vastly richer country.

The airport on Isla'Rosa was not modern, and that was being kind. That was another reason there was so much pressure on Laia to marry King Aristedes: for a much-needed financial injection into the economy. But

Laia was determined to haul Isla'Rosa into the modern age in her own way. Maddi admired that.

The plane touched down and Maddi could see an entourage of people and cars waiting. Cars with flags. Suddenly the magnitude of what she was doing hit her and she went clammy with nerves.

'Are you all right? You're very pale,' said the King.

Maddi nodded her head and smiled weakly. 'Might have been something I ate.'

King Aristedes all but snorted derisively. 'That wouldn't surprise me.'

He was standing up now, and he filled the space effortlessly. Maddi stood up too, and felt momentarily light-headed. Actually, contrary to what she'd just told King Aristedes, she hadn't had a solid meal in about forty-eight hours.

She must have swayed, or something, because suddenly her arm was in the King's hand. Not even his jacket could act as a barrier to the shock of his touch. Firm and strong.

His voice was gruff when he asked, 'Are you okay?'

Maddi nodded quickly. 'Fine…just stood up too fast.'

The King took his hand away and Maddi started to take off his jacket. 'You'll probably need this.'

'No.' His voice was sharp. 'Leave it on. There are clothes for you at the palace.'

Maddi frowned. 'But…you don't know my size.'

He looked at her. 'Of course I do. I have all your information, as you have mine.' His gaze swept her up and down. 'Although I'll admit you've changed a little in the four years since I've seen you. It's not a big deal—we can find clothes to fit you.'

Maddi felt his look like the lick of a flame over her skin. Yet she was pretty sure his words weren't complimentary. How humiliating that she found him attractive…

The discreet staff on the plane appeared and helped King Aristedes gather his things. The security men emerged again, from the front of the plane.

Maddi could see more people outside now. The clammy panic was back. She clutched the King's jacket around her like armour, as ineffectual as it was. She put her bag over her body. She felt very self-conscious.

Staff whispered into the King's ear and he looked stern again. Steps were brought to the plane. The door was opened. At the last moment Maddi remembered she had sunglasses and put them on.

King Aristedes stood at the door and gestured to her. 'Time to go.'

Maddi stepped into the doorway, glad of her sunglasses against the glare of the sun. She started to walk down the steps, very aware of her bare legs. The air was a lot cooler than it had been in the desert, but still pleasantly mild.

Out of the corner of her eye she spotted flashes of light and looked over. A crowd of photographers were just beyond a chain-link fence. She heard a curse behind her, and then there was a hand on her waist.

She almost lost her footing on the last step when King Aristedes said, 'Don't look at them. Come this way.'

She was bundled into the back of a sleek SUV with tinted windows and one of those little flags denoting a state car before she could think straight, and then they were moving out of the airport in a cavalcade, along wide roads lined with trees.

The roads soon brought them into the city, also called Santanger. It was a very substantial city, and an intriguing mix of old and new. The old part was full of small winding streets and honey-coloured stone buildings with terracotta tiles. Window boxes overflowing with flowers added bright pops of colour.

There was a massive cathedral overlooking the sea, Baroque in design and also of honey-coloured stone.

Glossy-looking boutiques on the winding road down to a marina told the story of wealth in this large island kingdom. And Maddi wasn't prepared for the vista opening up into a thoroughly modern part of the city, with soaring steel and glass buildings. It was the financial district. Which reminded Maddi that King Aristedes was renowned for his financial acumen and hosted one of the world's most prestigious global economic events on the island every year.

Apart from his inherited royal wealth, he was also one of the most independently wealthy men in the world. Not that Maddi cared a fig about that. The kind of wealth she valued was in getting to know her sister and finding a place she could really call home on Isla'Rosa.

The car turned away from the marina and went up a hill, out of the city. Soon they were driving under a massive stone arch guarded by men in uniform. Now they were clearly on private property.

Still, Maddi wasn't prepared when the cars drove into a massive courtyard with views straight out to the Mediterranean as far as the eye could see under a bright blue sky, not a cloud in sight. Water sparkled from an elaborate central fountain.

Her mouth dropped open. Beside her, King Aristedes said, 'Anyone would think you'd never been here before.'

She hadn't.

But of course Laia had, over the years, albeit infrequently.

Maddi clamped her mouth shut. Then, weakly, she said, 'It just…never fails to take my breath away.'

The car had come to a stop now, and King Aristedes stepped out. A man in what looked like a butler's uniform stepped forward and opened Maddi's door. She saw his eyes widen when she got out in her garish outfit.

Thankfully there didn't seem to be many other staff waiting for them, apart from the entourage from the airport and the security men. God only knew what they were thinking.

The palace up close was even more intimidating. A vast soaring entrance led into an open courtyard with another fountain. Off the inner courtyard there were numerous passageways.

A woman about her own age approached Maddi, smiling.

King Aristedes said, 'This is Hannah. She will take you to your rooms and show you where to find other clothes.'

Suddenly, at the prospect of the King leaving her to her own devices, Maddi felt very alone. 'Where are you going?'

King Aristedes looked at her as if she had two heads. Clearly he wasn't used to being questioned.

'As you can imagine, I have some work to take care of,' he said. 'We will have dinner together this evening. I will send for you.'

And then he walked away, flanked by about a dozen very officious-looking people.

Hannah said, 'Please come this way, Princess Laia.'

Maddi followed the girl through a warren of corridors, each more sumptuous than the last, with murals painted on the walls depicting scenes from around the island. They passed more inner courtyards with a distinctly Moorish influence. Evidently they shared the same marauding ancestors...

Then they took an elevator up a few floors. This level was hushed and even more opulent. It had to be where the bedrooms were. Hannah stopped outside some massive double doors and opened them with a flourish. Maddi stepped inside and it was like stepping into a dream.

A vast bedroom with a carpet so soft underfoot it felt like walking on air. A huge four-poster bed dressed in crisp white and blue linen.

The sleek bathroom featured two sinks, a walk-in shower, and a bath that oozed decadence, with shelves stocked with exclusive products.

There was also a lounge area, with a couch and a TV, books on shelves and all the latest glossy magazines spread out on a coffee table.

But the jewel in the crown of this room was the terrace, just beyond the open French doors. It was wide and generous, overflowing with colourful flowers from pots and planters trailing over the edge of the stone balcony. From there, Maddi had an unobstructed view out to sea, and far down below to where the city shone in the sunlight.

The palace spread out on either side of her...majestic. She could see formal gardens. An inviting pool. There was a larger terrace, presumably used for social gatherings but for now it was empty except for a peacock, which chose that exact moment to puff up its gloriously hued feathers, as if showing off just for Maddi.

She couldn't help smiling at the sight. And then she promptly stopped smiling when she thought of Laia.

Hannah cleared her throat behind her. 'Princess Laia, would you like some lunch?'

Maddi turned around just as her stomach rumbled. She made a face. 'Yes, please. I'm starving.'

Hannah's eyes widened. Maddi cursed silently. She had to remember she was pretending to be a princess. Well, she *was* actually a princess, but...

Her head started to throb lightly.

Hannah asked, 'Anything in particular?'

Maddi was about to say she'd eat everything and anything, but she stopped herself and said, 'A chicken salad would be lovely. With some bread. And fruit... and cheese. If that's okay?'

Hannah smiled. 'Not a problem. I'll return shortly. Please help yourself to whatever clothes you like in the dressing room. They're part of your trousseau from the King.'

Maddi had almost forgotten she was still in the

King's jacket, which reached only to the top of her thighs.

Hannah left and she went into the dressing room. It was huge and stuffed with clothes as far as the eye could see. And shoes and jewellery.

Maddi touched the iridescent colours of an evening gown. It shimmered as it moved slightly. She let go, afraid she might dirty it. With a growing sense of futility she searched in vain for some more casual clothes—jeans and a T-shirt, or athleisure wear.

Eventually she found a loose pair of trousers and a silk shirt. She opened the drawers and gasped when she saw the wispiest items of underwear. She pulled out a bra and it almost floated away it was so delicate. She grew hot at the thought of the King approving such purchases.

But of course he'd be too busy to bother himself with such things. He'd probably given someone a brief and they'd researched Princess Laia. Because all of these items were definitely suited to her sister more than to Maddi.

Maddi's style ran in a more eclectic direction. And she definitely needed more support from her underwear. Especially if that censorious look from the King on the plane was anything to go by. Just thinking of it again made her skin prickle and warmth bloom between her thighs.

These bras wouldn't go near fitting her, so she'd have to do without. She grabbed underwear and the shirt and trousers, and slipped out of her own clothes and into the new ones. They felt as light as air against her skin. She tied the ends of the shirt around her waist.

Hannah returned with a delicious lunch and left it on the table on the terrace. Maddi ate it with relish and savoured the view.

And then she thought of Laia and felt guilty. She got her phone out of her bag—it had been turned off since she got on the plane. She switched it on and there were numerous messages from Laia.

Are you okay? Where are you?

You're completely crazy, you know that?

Thank you, Mads, you've saved my life...

Where are you? Please let me know you're okay...

Maddi smiled and texted back.

I'm fine. We came straight to Santanger. The King has no idea I'm not you...yet. I hope this gives you enough time to get away...let me know where you are. By the way, I'm wearing clothes from your 'trousseau'. I hope you don't mind! I miss you! xx

Maddi sent the message and waited. Nothing. She presumed Laia must be travelling and put the phone down.

She sat looking at the view for a few more minutes, sipping her water, and then she started to feel restless.

She wanted to explore, but she wasn't sure if she was allowed to roam around. But then…she wasn't a prisoner, was she? Why shouldn't she explore the palace a little bit?

CHAPTER THREE

ARI WAS STANDING in his formal office at the palace. He'd showered and changed and allowed himself to feel a sense of satisfaction at having finally tracked his errant fiancée down.

But something about that niggled at him. It had been a little bit too…easy. His mouth thinned. If you discounted the fact that he'd had to fly to a remote desert to find her.

He went over to his French doors and opened them, the view of Santanger laid out below him never failing to make his blood surge with pride. He put his hands on the stone wall of the terrace and breathed in the familiar scents of his home—wild herbs, native flowers and the very distinctive salty tang of the sea.

He didn't take his inheritance for granted for a moment. Unlike his father, who had seen it as some sort of God-given right.

Maybe if his father hadn't displayed such feet of clay Ari might have been the same. But from an early age he'd known that his father was much closer to the earth than to God.

He'd witnessed the tawdry reality of his father's very

earthly desires—namely for other women. So he'd always had a sense that he didn't want to insult the people of Santanger by being a hypocrite—presenting the facade of a happy royal family when in reality it had been anything but.

Ari wasn't perfect by any means, but when it came to him marrying for the sake of his country he would do so with the utmost integrity. He would not be unfaithful. He would not do that to his Queen. He'd witnessed his own mother crumble and become a shell of a person. Belittled and made insecure.

She'd married for love and she'd never got over the betrayal of that dream. Ari could only be grateful that he'd learnt early in life that such a fantasy didn't exist.

Maybe for normal people. But not for people like him. Or Princess Laia.

Something caught the corner of his eye and he looked down to his left. As if conjured out of his thoughts, Princess Laia was walking around a courtyard, stopping to sniff flowers.

She'd changed into a shirt and loose trousers, and she was… Ari squinted…*barefoot?* A flash of heat went through him before he could stop it. She'd pulled her hair up into a loose knot and tendrils fell down around her face.

She'd always seemed neat to him before. Somehow fastidious. Here, with her shirt tied around her slim waist, she looked like a student who'd wandered in from outside the palace. As he watched, one of the palace dogs came into the courtyard, big and shaggy, of indeterminate breed.

He tensed. He knew Princess Laia had an aversion

to dogs because her father had been attacked by one as a small child. Ari had never noticed dogs in or around the castle on Isla'Rosa on his few visits over the years—understandable, if a little regrettable, because he himself loved dogs.

The dog ambled along behind an unsuspecting Princess Laia. Ari's hands gripped the wall. He didn't fear for her safety, only that she might get a fright. But, as if sensing the dog, she turned around and immediately dropped to her knees to greet him with smiles and soft words. Like any other dog-lover. Except Princess Laia was not a dog-lover—unless she'd had some kind of immersion therapy since he'd last seen her.

Ari frowned. He could distinctly remember her visiting Santanger when she was younger, with her father, and how they'd both tensed when the palace dogs had appeared. He'd had to have them put in the palace kennels until the visit was over. But Laia was crooning over this dog now, and scratching behind his ears.

A cold finger traced down Ari's spine as a suspicion started to form in his head. A suspicion that he couldn't even fully name yet. Just a feeling. He turned away from the view and went back to his desk, which was covered with newspapers and grainy paparazzi photos. He'd been about to throw them all in the bin—part of his efforts to track down Princess Laia that he no longer required. Except…maybe he did.

He pushed the papers and photos aside, growing more frustrated when he couldn't find what he was looking for—he wasn't even sure what he was looking for—but suddenly there it was.

A picture of Princess Laia in Central Park in Manhattan with another girl. Named under the photo as merely 'a friend'. They were arm in arm, heads together. Clearly close. And also…far more intriguingly…very physically similar. In fact they could almost be twins.

Similar height and build. Except the 'friend' was a little curvier. Both had long, wavy dark hair. They were wearing sunglasses, but Ari sat down now and searched online for a better image of Princess Laia. A formal photo popped up, showing very clearly that her eyes were a striking shade of green. To his shame, he couldn't have said for certain what colour her eyes were before. But now he could.

The woman he'd just brought to Santanger did not have green eyes. They weren't far off—a kind of hazel—but they weren't this very distinctive green.

The cold finger tracing down his spine became a burning sensation. Anger. When she'd been in Manhattan that time, he'd interrupted a trip to South America and had flown in at short notice to try and meet her. But when he'd arrived she'd already departed, leaving a paltry message of apology, saying that something had come up. Once again slipping through his fingers like mercury.

Another picture caught his eye. It was the grainy paparazzi photo of Princess Laia in the desert that had pinpointed her location for the first time in months. When Ari had read the caption under the photo his patience had snapped: *Is Party Princess Laia ever going to settle down?*

What he hadn't noticed until now was the same 'friend' with her in the picture. Arm in arm again.

Ari knew it now with cold certainty. The woman

currently in his palace, wearing clothes from the trousseau he'd bought for his fiancée, was *not* Princess Laia. No wonder she'd seemed so different. So if she wasn't the Princess, then who the hell was she? And where on earth—literally—was Princess Laia?

He picked up his mobile phone and made a call to his younger brother. He was grim. 'Dax? I need you to do something for me...'

'Princess Laia? The King is ready for you to meet him for dinner. If you'd follow me, please?'

Maddi felt unaccountably nervous. When she'd come back to the suite after exploring earlier she'd thought she might be tired enough to nap a little, but she'd been restless.

She wasn't used to just doing...nothing. Waiting around.

She and her mother had received a modest level of financial support from her father the King. Her mother probably could have got more, but she'd been too proud to ask for it.

It had been enough to give Maddi a good education, but not so much that they hadn't had to work for their keep. Her mother had worked as a receptionist for the local doctor in the small town outside Dublin where they'd lived. And Maddi had taken part-time jobs to help out from a young age. So she was used to working. To being active.

That was why she'd asked Laia if she could be her lady-in-waiting. It gave her something to do.

She followed Hannah down endless labyrinthine corridors, wondering if she should be slightly insulted that

King Aristedes had put so much space between himself and his 'fiancée'? But then they stopped abruptly at a set of double doors at the end of a corridor. There were guards outside. Stony-faced. They made Maddi want to try and make them smile, like she did with the guards on Isla'Rosa, but she controlled herself.

She suddenly felt self-conscious about what she was wearing, but it was too late. Hannah had knocked on the doors and the guards were opening them. Hannah stood back to let her into what was clearly the private apartment of King Aristedes, and the formal splendour of the foyer area alone told Maddi that she was dressed completely inappropriately.

What the hell was she wearing now?

Any thoughts Ari had had about confronting this stranger pretending to be Princess Laia dissolved in a rush of white-hot lust.

She was standing in his reception area and his mind couldn't even compute what she was wearing.

Black liquid trousers clung lovingly to long shapely legs.

Leather, Ari, it's called leather, supplied an atom of his brain that was still functioning.

The trousers showcased a very lush but firm bottom.

Blood rushed to every erogenous zone before he could stop it.

Above the waist she wore a black silky top overlaid with lace that highlighted her curvy but toned physique. And those amazing breasts.

His mouth went dry. She looked as if she wasn't wearing a bra—*again.*

Her hair was down, wavy and untamed. He could see that she wasn't wearing much make-up, but she didn't need it. Like Princess Laia, she had a natural beauty and stunning bone structure.

At least she was wearing shoes this time, even if they were spindly high-heeled sandals that added inches to her height. Which would put her even closer to his mouth.

Basta. Enough.

This woman, whoever she was, was intent on making a total fool out of him and she would be punished for that. And, *worse*, for making him want her.

He willed the lust in his body down to a dull throb and stepped forward out of the shadows.

'Princess Laia, thank you for joining me.'

Maddi started and turned towards where the King's voice had come from. A door leading out of the reception area. He looked mouthwateringly handsome, wearing dark trousers and a white shirt open at the neck.

He came towards her and she had to stop herself from moving back. Not because he intimidated her—but because of her own reaction. Her pulse was suddenly thundering, her skin prickling all over with awareness.

'King Aristedes.'

She suddenly wondered if she should curtsey, but maybe it was a bit late for protocol.

He stopped and held out a hand, indicating to the room beyond. 'Please, come in.'

She walked ahead of him, a little wobbly in the high heels, very aware of him behind her. The room she entered was vast, and had stunning views straight out to sea. French doors were open and a light breeze brought in scents of the island—wild flowers and the sea. Intoxicating.

The room was as opulent as the rest of the palace but also surprisingly not as decadently decorated as she had imagined it might be for a monarch. It was almost minimalist in style, with a few pieces of furniture and some abstract art on the walls. Maddi liked the unfussiness of it.

'And, please, I think there is no need for formalities. Call me Aristedes.'

Maddi turned around. Her breath hitched at just how gorgeous he was against this backdrop. Tall and vital and *sexy*.

Somehow she found her voice. 'Okay… Aristedes.' It felt unbelievably decadent, just saying his name.

He asked, 'Would you like a drink?'

He walked over to a drinks cabinet with that loose-limbed grace. For the life of her Maddi couldn't understand why Laia thought this man was staid…boring. He oozed a dynamic energy that made her skin prickle and her blood thunder.

He looked at her. Her mind was blank. Wiped clean because he was so distracting.

Drink, supplied a helpful voice. He'd asked her if she wanted a drink.

She was losing it. She wasn't sure what she should ask for, but the thought of something to take the edge off her self-consciousness sounded good. 'What are you having?'

He looked a little surprised by her question. 'A small whisky.'

Impetuously she said, 'I'll have the same.'

He brought over a tumbler with rich dark golden alcohol covering the bottom. She took it from him and sniffed it appreciatively.

She looked up. 'Scotch?'

He took a sip and nodded. 'How did you know?'

'My—' Maddi stopped. She'd been about to say, *My stepfather is an aficionado.* 'I took an interest on a trip to Scotland once.' She mentally crossed her fingers, hoping that Laia had been on a trip to Scotland.

Aristedes said, 'Ah, yes, I think you went there with your father?'

Maddi made a non-committal sound and took a sip, hoping he'd move on. The drink was fiery and immediately warming.

The sun was starting to set outside and the sky was turning a golden pink. Entranced, Maddi walked over and stood at the open French doors, beyond which there was a balcony and then nothing but a precipitous drop to the crashing sea below.

She sensed him coming close behind her.

She said, with genuine emotion, 'I would never get tired of this view.'

The similar sunsets on Isla'Rosa were also spectacular.

'I always had the impression that you were eager to travel and see the world beyond your own country. You've certainly spent little enough time on Isla'Rosa since your father died.'

Maddi tensed. Out of her and Laia, she was definitely more of a home bird. Laia—apart from trying to promote an image of a globe-trotting socialite—did have more of a wanderlust.

Maddi avoided his eye and looked out to the view again. She shrugged minutely. 'I'm young. I knew I would only have a finite amount of time before my ability to travel freely would be curtailed.'

A sound from behind them made Maddi turn around. There was a butler in uniform.

He bowed his head. 'Dinner is served, Your Majesty.'

'Thank you, Felipe.'

Aristedes stood back and said, 'This way, please.'

Maddi followed the butler and sent up silent thanks that Aristedes hadn't had a chance to pursue that last line of conversation, presumably relishing the chance to vent his ire about having to chase down his elusive fiancée.

Felipe led them into a relatively small private dining room. It was more elaborately decorated than the first room, in a rococo style. A table was set with a white linen tablecloth and silver service. Crystal glasses. More French doors were open, allowing that soft fragrant breeze to enter the room. There was another small balcony outside.

They sat down at the table and Maddi put the clutch bag she'd brought with her on the corner of the table. At the last minute she hadn't known what to bring, so she'd just stuffed her phone into the bag.

The butler left and the King took his napkin and flicked it open before laying it on his lap. Maddi locked eyes with him and for a moment saw something that made a little shiver go down her spine. *He knows.* But then whatever she'd thought she'd seen was gone and she robustly told herself she imagined it.

She put her own napkin across her lap. 'The style of these two rooms is very different…is there a reason for that?' she asked.

A shadow passed across Aristedes's face, but it was so fleeting Maddi thought she might have imagined it.

He said, 'I had the palace redecorated throughout on the death of my father.'

Maddi was about to ask, *When was that?* but as Laia she should know.

She took a quick gulp of water. 'I like what you've done. It's very…elegant. But this room is different.'

That was an understatement. She looked up now to see a mural on the ceiling—cherubs and clouds and voluptuous women.

'This room was my mother's favourite. When it came to it, I couldn't change it.'

Maddi looked at him. 'You were close?'

His face became expressionless. 'Close enough.'

On that succinct and distinctly chilly response the butler and some maids appeared with their starters. A light salad of sweet pear with walnuts and parmesan. White wine was poured and it tasted light and slightly fizzy.

'That was delicious,' Maddi said after she'd cleaned her plate.

'All locally grown.'

'As is most of the food on Isla'Rosa,' Maddi felt compelled to point out.

Every weekend one of her favourite things to do was to go down to the farmers' market and buy ingredients to cook. She'd been teaching Laia how to cook recently.

Her heart squeezed. Where was she? Had she got

away somewhere safe? There hadn't been another text message yet.

Aristedes lifted his glass in salute. 'We are very lucky to have such wonderful resources.'

He sounded faintly mocking. But then Maddi wondered if she was hearing things. Being paranoid. The staff came back and removed their plates, then returned with the main course—a light and flavoursome beef stew.

'You have a good appetite.'

Maddi put down her fork and felt a dull flush climb into her face. Her endless capacity for food was an affectionate joke between her and her sister.

'I like food.'

Maddi knew she sounded defensive. And she knew she wasn't exactly behaving like a delicate princess. What she wanted to know was how they had got the beef so tender and tasty. Had they marinated it?

'When you were here with your father as a teenager you were a vegetarian. Obviously that was a phase?'

Maddi went panicky and cold inside as she thought furiously of when she'd last seen Laia eating meat. And then she relaxed. It had been a week ago—she'd eaten a burger. Well, she'd eaten half and Maddi had eaten the other half.

'Yes, it was a phase,' Maddi said with some relief, and picked up her glass of wine to take another sip.

'And have you always had that gap between your front teeth? I've never noticed it before.'

Maddi almost spat out her wine, but somehow managed to keep it in her mouth and swallow it without looking as if she was choking. She did have a gap in her front teeth. Not hugely prominent, but enough of a feature to be noticeable.

She decided to try and brazen it out. 'Are you sure you've never noticed it before? We haven't exactly been... close.' A frisson of awareness skittered over her skin.

Aristedes shook his head, eyes on her. On her mouth. 'I think I would have remembered a feature like that. It's...noticeable.'

'Maybe my teeth are just...growing apart?'

'In that case perhaps you should see the palace dentist?'

Maddi wanted to squirm. 'I'm sure it's nothing to worry about. Teeth shift all the time. I remember when I had braces—'

'I don't remember you with braces.'

He knew, and he was toying with her.

The suspicion lodged in her head, making Maddi even more trenchant. 'I didn't visit here all that often, I had them as a young teenager.'

Laia had told her she'd always tried to duck out of visiting with her father over the years.

'Clearly I should have paid more attention.'

His tone was perfectly bland, but Maddi looked at him suspiciously. He watched her lazily. She had an impression of a big jungle cat, toying with a morsel of food. The air around them felt closer. Heavier.

The staff came back, breaking the weird moment, and cleared the plates.

The butler asked, 'Would Princess Laia like some dessert? Tea or coffee?'

'Or perhaps a digestif?' the King interjected.

Maddi looked at her wine glass. It was empty. The

wine together with the whisky was already having an effect. The thought of dessert was tempting, but she didn't want to draw attention to her appetite again and she knew Laia didn't have a sweet tooth like her.

She shook her head and smiled at Felipe. 'Just a coffee would be lovely, thank you.'

'I'll have the same. Thank you, Felipe.'

Alone with him again, Maddi felt pinned under Aristedes's gaze. She stood up and went to the balcony, looking out over the sea. It was dramatic and awesome. She looked down. And not a little terrifying. A suspicion slid into her mind. Had he brought her here on purpose, because he was going to expose her and then tip her into the sea as punishment?

Felipe returned with coffee and biscuits and Maddi went back to the table. She tried to ignore the tension once they were alone again and busied herself with milk and sugar.

'Sweet tooth?' Aristedes enquired.

Maddi cursed herself and put back the second spoonful of sugar. 'Sometimes. But not in general, no.'

Then he said, almost idly, 'I'm glad you're finally here. We've been waiting a lifetime for this moment.'

Laia had. Maddi, up until relatively recently, had been living a very normal life.

Well, normal except for the fact that she hadn't had a boyfriend yet. Or a casual lover. Or a one-night stand. All the boys she'd met had seemed like…boys. Not men. She hadn't been remotely interested. She hadn't felt anything.

Until she'd seen Aristedes climb out of his car in the desert in his ridiculously out of place three-piece suit.

Maddi cursed her hormones for being triggered by the worst person in the world for her to develop a crush on. Literally the worst. The most inappropriate.

She tried to focus on what he'd said. 'I... Yes, I guess we have been waiting a lifetime.'

'And only another two weeks until you will become Queen of Santanger and of your own kingdom.'

'Of which you will also become King.'

He dipped his head. 'As has been the agreement since you were born and since I was eight years old.'

Curiosity got the better of Maddi for a moment. 'And it really doesn't bother you that this is a marriage purely for business purposes?'

'And succession purposes. We will have children, Laia.'

Heat bloomed between Maddi's thighs at the thought of making those children. She pressed her legs together under the table. She was not here to make children with this man!

He went on, 'Not to mention for all the very good reasons of promoting peace and fostering economic growth on Isla'Rosa. You have nothing to lose.'

'Only my autonomy—my country's autonomy.' Maddi knew Laia would have wanted her to say that.

'*We* don't get to have autonomy. We have responsibilities to our people.'

Maddi leaned forward. 'But don't you want to be happy? I mean, I'm no idealistic romantic, but surely a marriage will thrive better if there is a sense of companionship and...' She stopped.

He arched a brow. 'And?'

Maddi's face was hot now. 'Mutual...attraction?'

'Oh, I think we have something we can work with.'

Maddi balked. 'You do?' It came out as a squeak.

Aristedes stood up on the other side of the table and held out a hand. This was heading into territory that Maddi had no idea how to navigate. Reluctantly, but also with an electric buzz in her blood, she put her hand in his and let him help her up. He moved closer, so they were standing only inches apart by the table.

Maddi couldn't look away from his eyes. They were dark, but she could see golden lights, very deep. Like fires burning. She was burning too, inside. She couldn't breathe.

Aristedes lifted her hand and held it close enough to his mouth for her to feel his breath. Her breasts felt heavy, and something completely new and alien coiled and writhed, alive in her lower body. She felt hungry, but it wasn't for food.

His mouth was…sinful. Firm. Sculpted. She desperately wanted him to touch his lips to her skin.

But he didn't bring her hand to his mouth. He said softly, 'Exactly how long are you planning on keeping up this charade?'

The heat haze in Maddi's body went cold. 'I'm sorry…what did you say?' Maybe she'd misheard him?

He said, slowly and distinctly, 'We definitely have something we can work with—which would be very convenient if you were, in fact, my fiancée, Princess Laia. But we both know you're not, are you?'

He knew. Had he known all along? Since when? The plane?

Maddi's brain went into freefall. She tried to pull

her hand back but the King held on. Not too tightly. But tightly enough.

He said, 'Who are you?'

Desperately scrabbling for time to think, Maddi asked, 'When did you know?'

He looked at her for a long moment and then let her hand go, pacing away to the French doors. Ridiculously, Maddi felt almost rejected. She held her hand to her chest.

He turned around and looked at her, and at her hand. Sharply, he said, 'Did I hurt you?'

'No, not at all… I just…'

She dropped her hand. How could she explain that when he touched her it had burned, but not in a bad way?

He folded his arms across his chest, but that only made her notice the way his muscles pushed against his shirt. 'So, who are you?'

Maddi swallowed. 'I'm Princess Laia's lady-in-waiting.'

'What's your name?'

Rapid-fire questions.

'Maddi Smith.'

'You look very alike.'

Maddi scrabbled to find an explanation. No way could she tell him she was Laia's half-sister. He would use the information to draw Laia out of hiding, or God knows what else.

'Have you never heard of doppelgangers? We're just very alike. My mother was from Isla'Rosa…' She stopped there.

'Did you grow up there?'

She shook her head. 'No, I grew up in Ireland.' To

stop him asking questions for a minute she repeated her own. 'When did you know?'

'I don't think you're really in any position to ask questions, are you?'

Maddi bit her lip and she saw his gaze move there. The air between them snapped and crackled.

He looked back up. Almost as if he couldn't help himself, he finally said, 'The dog. I saw you with the dog. I remembered Laia has a fear of them because of her father.'

Of course. Maddi had stopped to pet a dog one day, when she and Laia been walking somewhere, and she'd only noticed that Laia had turned to stone behind her after a few seconds. Laia had explained about her irrational fear. She wanted to like dogs, but her father's fear after being attacked as a young boy had seeped into her consciousness too, and she couldn't seem to let it go.

'So what happens now?' she asked.

Aristedes sat back on the wall of the balcony and Maddi felt her insides swoop as she thought of the perilous drop on the other side.

Before she could stop herself, she put out a hand, 'Could you not do that, please?'

He frowned. 'Do what?'

'Perch on the only thing between you and crashing to your death on the rocks below.'

He didn't move. 'These walls have been here since the Middle Ages and they'll outlast us.'

Something about her face must have transmitted how terrified she was and he stood up. 'What happens now? What happens now is that you tell me where Laia is.'

Maddi's hand dropped back to her side. 'I don't know.'

The King's mouth compressed. 'I don't suppose you

went through all this just to turn around and give me her location.'

Maddi almost felt sorry for him. 'No. But the truth is that I have no idea where she is. Honestly. All I was doing was giving her a chance to escape.'

'Escape the life she knew she was destined for? A life of privilege?'

'She wants more. And she wants to be Queen of her own country.'

Aristedes, clearly frustrated, ran a hand through his hair, messing it up. 'She *will* be Queen of her own country.'

'Yes, but it'll become just a smaller state—part of Santanger. With the best will in the world, you can't guarantee that it won't. She doesn't want to be Queen of here.'

'I'm afraid she doesn't really have a choice. Where is she?'

Maddi was beginning to feel annoyed. 'I told you—I don't know.'

At that moment there was a *ping* from behind her. She went cold. *Her phone.*

She turned around and grabbed her bag. She opened it and looked at the screen. All she could see without unlocking it was the start of a message from Laia:

Mads! It's all cool. I'm safe and very far away in...

She couldn't see the rest of the message without unlocking the phone.

She looked up. Aristedes was in front of her, holding out his hand.

'That's a message from Laia, isn't it? Give it to me.'

No way.

Maddi clutched the phone tightly in her hand and dropped the bag to the floor. She slowly moved sideways around the King and backed towards the open French doors.

He kept his hand out and turned to face her. He said warningly, 'Maddi…the phone.'

But Maddi could feel the air behind her now, and before she lost her nerve she turned around and hurled the phone out into the sky that was now dusky.

She wondered vaguely how long it would take for the phone to reach the rocks and smash to bits. Or had she thrown it hard enough to land all the way in the sea?

CHAPTER FOUR

AN HOUR LATER, Ari was still pacing back and forth in the private dining room, filled with so many volatile emotions and, worse, *desire*, that he didn't know what to unpick first.

He couldn't get the image of Laia—*blast it!*—Maddi out of his mind's eye, when she'd been standing in front of him with huge eyes and biting her lip. In that moment, in spite of her deception, all he'd wanted to do was cup her face in his hands and kiss that treacherous mouth until she was soft and pliable in his arms and—

Mierda.

He'd never been so distracted by his hormones. And for it to be happening now was particularly galling. He needed all his wits about him. Maddi had been returned to her suite of rooms with a guard outside. He couldn't afford to have her disappear now. Not when she was his only link to Princess Laia.

He couldn't believe she'd thrown her mobile phone into the sea. But there would be other ways for them to communicate. He just had to make sure he knew when they did.

He left the dining room and went back to his offices

and paced some more there. He was about to call for his senior advisor, but at the last moment he stopped when something occurred to him.

He was the only person who knew about this. Who knew that Maddi Smith was *not* Princess Laia.

The last thing he needed now was a tabloid frenzy if the story slipped out. He had his brother Dax on the case, tracking down Laia. There was no one he trusted more in the world. Dax would find her and return her to Santanger.

In the meantime…everyone believed Princess Laia was here. And that their engagement was progressing. So why shouldn't he take advantage of that situation? He would have to delay the wedding preparations that had been put into motion as soon as he'd found Laia— *Maddi*. But he would just explain it as wanting to extend their engagement for a short time. After all, they'd spent hardly any time together.

As it was, the specific details of the wedding date etc hadn't been made public yet, out of a very small but real risk of rebel elements using the wedding to stoke up unrest in the kingdoms. So, if anything, he could use this to his advantage now.

Clearly when the real Princess Laia did arrive they *would* have some things to discuss. As much as he would have liked simply to switch the fake Princess for the real one, he could recognise that that wasn't practical. Laia had certainly made it clear that she wasn't coming into this marriage willingly.

So, no matter what happened the wedding was on hold. But not derailed. Not as long as he had 'Princess Laia' here, sticking to the engagement schedule.

Until the real Princess got here, no one would be

any the wiser, and they could get on with planning the wedding.

The thought of Laia shirking her duty sent fresh anger through him. They didn't have the luxury of shirking their duty. He didn't. And neither did she. Their marriage was the next step in the process of making Santanger even stronger. Creating a new royal dynasty. Creating the next generation of rulers.

The fact that it would also ensure lasting peace between their two countries was an added bonus. In an unstable world, people wanted assurances of longevity and stability and their marriage would permanently defuse any of the small, but lingering rebel elements in both kingdoms. It was time to let the past go for good and move into a new harmonious future.

Ari had never entertained any notions of marrying for love—he'd witnessed what love had done to his mother. Made her weak and bitter. And all the while his father had shown his callous disregard, taking lovers into his private rooms while his wife, his Queen, had self-destructed.

Something Maddi had said came back to him...

'But don't you want to be happy? I mean, I'm no idealistic romantic, but surely a marriage will thrive better if there is a sense of companionship...'

He didn't disagree with that sentiment entirely. He knew exactly what he expected from his marriage to Princess Laia. Mutual respect. Integrity. And, yes... ideally, companionship. From which they would create a stable union and a secure foundation for their heirs. With none of the drama and emotion and histrionics he'd witnessed in his parents.

But as for happiness…? Happiness wasn't something Ari had ever expected or craved. It wasn't something he needed. He would find happiness in knowing that things were proceeding as they should. As they'd been planned. Meticulously.

And right now he was *not* happy.

An image of Maddi popped into his head…standing there so defiantly after she'd thrown her phone away. Tall and strong and curvaceous. Like some sort of amazon warrior. She'd looked regal in that moment. *And sexy as hell.*

Ari shook his head to dispel the image and the thought. He would control this entire situation—including his rogue hormones. She would not get away with this audacity.

But there was one thing he needed to attend to, with possibly the only other person in the world he trusted as much as his brother. An old friend who now ran a security company that provided his protection and that of every other high-ranking individual on the planet.

After a small amount of chitchat, Ari said, 'If I give you a name, can you investigate and ask no questions?'

'Of course. Consider it done.'

'Thank you.' Ari gave his friend the name and terminated the call. If there was anything he needed to know about Maddi Smith, his friend Antonio Chatsfield would unearth it.

The following morning

'You are welcome here as my guest, until such time as Laia arrives. And I can assure you she will. I have someone looking for her right now.'

'Who?' asked Maddi.

She hadn't slept well last night—unsurprisingly. But not just because Aristedes had found out about the deception. No, her fractured sleep and dreams had been populated by very disturbing images of him punishing her for her transgression by hauling her into his hard body and kissing her until she was dizzy and molten. Senseless.

She'd been woken early by Hannah, who had told her the King would join her for breakfast in her suite. A small dining table had been set up in the sitting area.

She hadn't known what to expect of the King this morning but he seemed perfectly sanguine. She didn't trust it.

'Who, what?' he asked as he plucked a grape from the fruit bowl and popped it into his mouth.

Maddi couldn't help but feel slightly jealous of the grape as those firm lips closed around it. He was wearing a light blue shirt today, and dark trousers. Beard neat and trim. Hair thick and pushed back from his face, revealing all its hard-boned beauty. He really was spectacular.

'Maddi?'

She blinked. She was losing it. 'Who have you sent to look for Laia?'

'The best person for the job. My younger brother, Crown Prince Dax.'

Maddi's eyes widened. If there was anyone in the world Laia disliked more than Aristedes—and, to be fair, she didn't *not* like him…she just didn't want to marry him and thought he was too serious—it was his

brother. The renowned playboy, the 'spare' heir, Crown
Prince Dax de Valle y Montero.

Maddi had been surprised at the level of Laia's dis-
like for the man. Whenever she saw pictures of him with
yet another beautiful model, stepping out of a club, or
lounging on a yacht, she would make dismissive com-
ments about his lack of a work ethic and/or his lack of
responsibility to his duties.

It was ironic, really. Laia was perceived as being not
unlike Crown Prince Dax, but in reality she couldn't be
more different. Maddi felt sorry for the guy if he did
manage to find Laia.

'Anything you'd like to share?' asked Aristedes.

He'd obviously noticed her reaction.

Maddi shook her head and wiped her face clean of
expression. 'No, nothing at all.'

She put half a croissant in her mouth to stop herself
from blurting anything out. She had a habit of speaking
whatever was in her head. It was a miracle Aristedes
hadn't figured her out as an imposter sooner.

When she'd swallowed the croissant, she said, 'What
if I don't want to stay here as your guest?'

'But I insist.'

'You mean, you're going to keep me here as a prisoner?'

He made a face. 'So dramatic… Nothing like that.
Considering the fact that you've offered yourself up in
place of Laia, I'm merely accepting your offer.'

'Offer…? I haven't offered anything.'

'The moment you stood in front of me and let me believe you were Princess Laia, the offer was made. Everyone here believes you are Princess Laia, and that's

how it shall remain until she assumes her rightful place by my side.'

Maddi went cold inside. She hadn't really thought ahead to what would happen if she was found out. 'You can't keep me here against my will.'

'Oh, you'll stay, and it'll be your choice—as it was your choice to come here. You'll be doing what's best for Princess Laia and Isla'Rosa and her future marriage.'

'How's that, exactly?'

'I could expose you in a second. That would cause lurid headlines for Princess Laia and potentially draw her out of her hiding place… But it would also be a scandal for me, and I don't particularly relish adverse headlines—I never have.'

No, he hadn't. Contrary to his younger brother's behaviour, since Aristedes had ascended to the throne on his father's death he'd always stayed within the margins of propriety and respectability. If he took lovers they were from a pool of socially acceptable peers. The moment it looked as if things might be getting serious, he cut things off. He'd never jeopardised the wedding pact with Princess Laia. As much as she'd wished he would.

But he hadn't lived as a monk, and along with his brother he'd garnered a reputation as a skilful lover. His reputation, of course, was less lurid than Dax's— whose lovers invariably kissed and told. In vivid detail.

He went on, 'There's no need for anyone to ever know about this. You'll keep up the fiction that you are Princess Laia, and you will accompany me to all the events she was scheduled to attend during her time here.'

'But…' Maddi's brain felt foggy. 'What if someone notices I'm not her?'

'They won't get close enough to see the small differences. You fooled me, and I've met her. You really are very similar.'

'Doppelgangers,' muttered Maddi.

'When Laia gets here no one will be any the wiser and we can all get on with our lives.'

His calm self-assurance made Maddi feel prickly—or was it his insistence that as soon as Laia arrived she'd be jettisoned in favour of her half-sister, even when there was this palpable…*thing* between them, like a current of electricity?

'You're very certain it will all work out in your favour.'

'Things generally do.'

That made her even pricklier. 'And what's to stop me from leaking the truth and flushing Laia out so I can let her know what your plan is?'

His gaze narrowed on her. 'Do you really want to see your future Queen embroiled in more salacious headlines than the ones referring to her insatiable appetite for partying? No matter what happens, she turns twenty-five soon and she will be Queen. Do you think this stunt will really inspire her people to believe she's ready to rule?'

Maddi was silent. Maybe he had a point. Laia's privy council knew that she was hard-working and hadn't let her responsibilities slide, in spite of her social life. And the people of Isla'Rosa were fiercely loyal to their Crown Princess. But negative press so close to her birthday and the coronation could be damaging.

Then Aristedes said, 'Not to mention the peace agreement. Do I need to remind you of what's at stake if the marriage doesn't go ahead?'

Maddi felt sick. 'But there are other options…'

'Options that I'm not willing to entertain when this dynastic marriage will comprehensively ensure peace for generations to come. To be perfectly frank, whether or not Laia becomes Queen of Isla'Rosa before or after our marriage isn't really all that important, but the marriage must take place.'

Maddi felt defeated by his determination. He'd obviously come to terms with the fact that Laia might be crowned Queen of Isla'Rosa before they married, but he still expected her to marry him. He didn't know Laia had other plans, but Maddi had met him now and could appreciate how persuasive he was.

Laia could still find herself getting backed into a corner where she might feel she had no option but to go ahead with the marriage. What if he refused to discuss peace plans unless they were married? If anything, the stakes would be even higher if she'd already been crowned Queen! Then all of this would have been for nothing.

Maddi longed to warn Laia. But she had no way of contacting her now, after throwing her phone away. She couldn't reveal to Aristedes Laia's plans for another route to peace—he would do something to thwart them. It was more urgent than ever that she do all she could to protect Laia and make sure she got to her birthday and the coronation. She had to trust that Laia had considered all this and knew what she was doing.

'Okay, I will agree to pose as Laia…until she is found.' Maddi crossed her fingers on her lap under the table.

The King's eyes flicked down. A muscle pulsed in his jaw. 'The table is made of glass, Maddi.'

She hadn't noticed. She went puce and uncrossed her fingers. 'I'm just saying that my priority is protecting her wishes, and if that means pretending to be her then so be it.'

'Don't worry. I have faith in my brother. He hasn't failed me yet.'

Maddi privately wondered how accurate that was, when the guy was never not partying, but she kept it to herself.

'So what happens now?'

He flicked another glance over her attire. She'd dressed in a hurry, pulling on a silk shirt and a pair of designer jeans. She'd had to go braless again, and the shirt was straining a little across her chest. Treacherously, she could feel the tips of her breasts pucker and tighten. She wanted to cross her arms, but didn't want to draw even more attention to the area.

Aristedes said briskly, 'I've postponed the wedding plans for now. My staff believe it's so that we can spend more time getting to know one another, so you'll be spared a wedding dress fitting. But I'll arrange for a stylist to order some more…suitable clothes. Then you'll be slotted into the schedule we had already arranged to introduce the people of Santanger to their future Queen.'

Maddi's heart palpitated. She tried desperately to stop images of herself trying on wedding dresses from forming in her head. 'Schedule…? That sounds busy.'

'It is,' agreed the King. 'There's an event most days, and you will need lessons in Santanger's history and etiquette. Laia would have known what to do, but you'll need all the help you can get.'

Suddenly Maddi realised that, whether she liked it or not, she was about to be thrown in at the deep end of being a princess. Her insides swooped sickeningly. She hadn't considered things would go this far...but there was no turning back now.

Two days later, Maddi's head throbbed from an overload of information and her body ached from being poked and prodded and waxed and buffed and pummelled. All in the name of transforming her into a sleeker version of her. Into Princess Laia.

She now had an entirely new wardrobe of clothes. Specifically to fit *her*. The wispy, floaty bras were gone and had been replaced by items a little more...supportive, but no less provocative or wispy. It was good to feel a little less exposed again.

She had just had a lesson in Santanger royal etiquette from one of the King's aides, and was now waiting for Hannah to take her to meet the King for lunch.

Maddi hadn't seen him in two days and she was embarrassingly nervous. Like a teenager, with butterflies swooping around her belly. She was wearing a sleeveless plain shift dress in dark caramel tones. It came to her knees, but had a discreet little slit up one side. She wore matching court shoes. She fidgeted in the dress. She felt as if she was going to an interview for a job in a bank.

She'd pulled her hair back earlier into a low ponytail—she'd had it trimmed yesterday, to take some of the unruly heaviness out—but now, in a fit of something rebellious, Maddi pulled her hair free and left it loose, falling around her shoulders.

There was a knock on the door. Hannah appeared. 'Princess Laia? If you'll come with me, please, the King is ready for you.'

Maddi dutifully followed Hannah who was quickly becoming her only real touchstone in this vast and dizzying place full of labyrinthine corridors, dead ends, and spiral staircases disappearing to who knew where—towers for impersonators?

Maddi almost slammed into Hannah's back before she realised they'd stopped outside a door. This was a different door from the one leading into Aristedes's private suite of rooms. Once again, guards were present. One of them opened the door, stepped in, announced Maddi and then stood back to let her enter.

She realised immediately that it must be his offices. Bright and airy. Surprisingly modern. She saw an anteroom to one side with desks and staff. A couple looked up curiously. She seemed to be in a reception area.

And then a door opened to her right and there he was, effortlessly filling the frame with his tall, powerful build. He looked slightly hassled. A little bit grim.

'Princess Laia, please come in.'

He stood back to let her pass and his scent washed over her and through her. Evocative and potent. His office was huge, with a separate seating area where there was a TV with a rolling news channel on mute. Floor-to-ceiling bookshelves filled one side, and vast windows looked out to the vista of the sea and the island on the other side.

There was a table set up for lunch. Aristedes gestured to it. 'Please, take a seat.'

Maddi did so, aware of his eyes on her as he sat down too. Would he approve of her slightly more put-together appearance? She sneaked a look at him and flushed. His dark eyes were boring into her.

'What is it? Do I not look the part? They spent hours working on me—'

'My brother has gone AWOL.'

Maddi felt a jolt of relief. She put her hands in her lap. 'Oh. Well, maybe he's gone to a party somewhere.'

Aristedes's expression darkened. 'What are you suggesting?'

Maddi refused to let him intimidate her. 'That he has a reputation for...such things.'

'He would not be distracted in this instance. Not if it's a request from me.'

Maddi shrugged minutely. 'Well, you know him better than me. I've never met him.'

Aristedes stood up and paced back and forth, muttering to himself—something about it not being like Dax to just disappear. Secretly, Maddi wondered if Laia had anything to do with it. Maybe he'd tracked her down and she'd managed to disable him in some way?

Aristedes turned around and glared at her. Maddi felt a very illicit throb of awareness.

'Are you sure you don't know anything about this?'

She lifted her hands. 'No phone. No means of communication.'

Aristedes made a sound of frustration and sat down

again, flicking out his napkin before laying it across his lap.

Maddi felt guilty then, and leaned forward. 'Don't worry. I'm sure he's okay.'

Aristedes made another sound—a snorting one. 'Oh, I don't doubt that. He can handle himself better than my most experienced security guards.'

A staff member came in with plates of salad, light and zesty, served with fresh crusty bread. Maddi's mouth watered, but she stopped herself from falling upon the food. She hadn't eaten much over the last two days, with all the lessons and fittings and beauty treatments.

When they were alone again she asked, 'You're close to your brother?'

He looked at her suspiciously for a moment before saying, 'Yes, very. It was just the two of us.'

'This must have been a fun place to grow up. Hide and seek could take days.'

As if she'd caught him by surprise, he said, 'We did have fun...but when we played hide and seek it was usually us hiding from our nanny or the security guards.'

Maddi smiled. She could imagine two dark-haired imps turning the hair of everyone around them grey. 'I bet you were handfuls.'

'We were—until I had to be prepared for inheriting the crown one day.'

'How old were you?'

'Eight.'

Maddi sucked in a breath. 'So young.'

His gaze narrowed on her. 'I was happy to bear that responsibility.'

'I can't imagine what that must have been like.'

She'd had a carefree childhood. Unlike Laia. And Aristedes. They had that in common. She felt a prick of jealousy and quickly quashed it.

'Do you have brothers and sisters?' Aristedes asked.

Maddi avoided his eye. 'I grew up an only child.' That was factual, at least.

Before he could quiz her on her meaning, their plates were cleared and main courses brought in. Sea bass in a delicious herb sauce with new potatoes and vegetables. Maddi concentrated on eating to avoid making conversation.

'You like your food. I don't remember Laia having such a healthy appetite.'

Maddi swallowed a mouthful and fought back a wave of self-consciousness. She wiped her mouth with the napkin. 'I appreciate food, yes. I enjoy cooking it too.'

He arched a brow. 'A cook and an impersonator? That's impressive.'

That stung. But it was a fair comment.

He went on, 'What else do you do? I have a feeling you could turn your hand to pretty much anything.'

Maddi was fairly sure he didn't mean that as a compliment. Self-consciousness struck again. 'I didn't go to university. I was never academically inclined. When I left school I went to work in Dublin in a…a casino.' She almost winced as she said this.

'As a croupier?'

She shook her head. 'No, a waitress.'

She shuddered slightly as she recalled the wandering hands of some of the male clients. Especially after a few drinks or winnings.

Quickly, she said, 'But I also worked in restaurants,

and as a nanny for a while. I'm an expert in cooking for kids of a certain age and convincing them that broccoli is fun to eat.'

Aristedes looked mildly horrified. Princess Laia *had* gone to university, to do a degree in international relations and economics. She was able to navigate a state dinner for up to a hundred people without breaking a sweat. *She* was obviously ideal to become the wife of King Aristedes. No wonder he was so intent on pursuing her.

For the first time in her life Maddi felt inadequate, when before she'd always held a certain amount of pride in her ability to jump into any situation and do well in spite of her lack of academic qualifications.

Feeling defensive, she asked, 'What did you do at university?'

He looked at her. 'I didn't go.'

'Oh? Why not?' Maybe he'd already had all the information. She wouldn't be surprised.

'My father died when I was eighteen and I became King. There was no time to go to university.'

'Did you want to go?'

'I had a place at Harvard. Yes, I would have loved it.'

Maddi's heart squeezed. He actually sounded wistful.

'What were you going to study?'

His mouth quirked slightly. 'Engineering.'

Maddi sat back. 'That's impressive.'

'I still did the degree. I just had to do it remotely. Here.'

'Not quite the same experience as living at a university and being relatively carefree for four years.'

'No. But then I was never destined for a carefree life.'

'Do you mind that your brother got to have that life and you didn't?'

He blinked. 'No, of course not. He has his own set of challenges that I have never faced.'

Like what? Maddi wanted to ask.

But their plates were being cleared now, and coffee was served with little delicious biscuits.

Ari cursed the woman opposite him. Her innocent questions were precipitating a slew of memories. One of which was particularly vivid. He'd been playing chase with Dax, the two of them scuffed and dusty. He remembered that his stomach had hurt from laughing. Suddenly he'd been hauled up by the back of his shirt to see his father's humourless chief advisor glaring at him.

'It's time for your lessons. You've been told you can't play in the palace like this any more. It's not seemly for the heir to the throne.'

Ari remembered the stone-like feeling sinking into his belly. All the happiness gone. The look of disappointment on Dax's face as Ari had been led away to the dusty and musty schoolroom.

Not a hugely traumatic memory, to be fair, but it had signalled the end of the only time in his life when he remembered being free. When he'd had his brother by his side all the time. Before they'd effectively been split up.

He remembered that had also been around the time that his parents' marriage had fractured in plain sight. He'd been told not long afterwards that a princess had been born in another country and that one day she would be his wife. The thought had terrified Ari as a child. Especially when he'd seen his own mother so upset and unhappy.

He'd vowed all the way back then, with a child's logic, that he would never cause his wife to be that unhappy. It was only as he'd grown up that he'd realised what that would mean. No emotion. No love. Because love only caused things like jealousy and insecurity and ultimately tragedy.

'What is it? I ask too many questions…is that it?'

Maddi's voice broke Ari out of the past. He looked at her and was surprised at the concern on her face. It made something shift inside him. What was he doing, sitting here having a surprisingly easy conversation with this woman who, together with Princess Laia, had thrown the marriage pact between Santanger and Isla'Rosa into complete disarray?

Today she looked…less wild. But no less beautiful. Because she *was* beautiful. More beautiful than he had initially given her credit for. Her bone structure was that of a classic beauty. High cheekbones. Firm jaw. Straight nose. Big eyes, beautifully framed by dark, arching brows and long, luxurious lashes.

She was also now wearing clothes that *fitted*, and in a colour that made her skin look golden and silky. The dress enhanced her curves without being provocative. Yet she was still provocative to him. Even though she wasn't wearing a shirt that strained over her very obviously braless breasts. Even though she wasn't barefoot.

He shook his head. 'It's fine. You didn't say anything that hasn't already been said a million times.'

She shrugged minutely. 'Okay.'

She dunked a biscuit into her coffee and popped it into her mouth, between those lush lips. He caught a glimpse of that maddening gap between her teeth. Everything about her seemed designed to get under his skin like a thorn and *itch*.

She pushed her hair behind her ear at that moment, and Ari caught a glimpse of something twinkling high on her ear.

He leaned forward. 'What is that?'

She looked at him, eyes amber and gold. 'What is what?'

He pointed. 'In your ear.'

Maddi touched it. 'It's a diamond stud.'

'It'll have to go.'

She looked crestfallen. 'It was a gift from someone…special.'

Ari immediately felt hot all over—and not with desire. With something far more volatile. 'A lover?'

She shook her head, making her glossy hair slip over her shoulders. It looked like burnished brown silk.

'No, just a friend.'

The volatility in Ari calmed a little. 'Like I said, you'll have to remove it. It's too…unconventional.'

She lifted her chin. 'Maybe a little unconventionality wouldn't be such a bad thing?'

The volatility was back. No one spoke like that to Ari. Yet, as much as it angered him, he hated to admit that he also found it…refreshing.

He said, '*If* you were Princess Laia I would be happy to pursue a conversation about the merits of unconventionality within the parameters of a royal marriage, but you're not. We have a function to attend this evening. Remove the stud.'

Now Maddi went pale. 'This evening? What event?'

He almost felt sorry for her. *Almost.* 'A garden party here at the palace. Relatively informal. To introduce you to some staff and members of parliament. Important people in Santanger society.'

A few hours after lunch Maddi was standing in front of a mirror in her bedroom, nerves coiling in her belly like restless snakes. She'd got used to dressing formally when working as Laia's lady-in-waiting, but she'd always been dressed to fade into the background, in muted colours.

Now she was dressed to stand out. It was a royal blue silk dress, loosely fitted and mid-length. Sleeveless. Deceptively simple, yet so elegant it took Maddi's breath away. It flowed and moved like air around her body.

She wore matching high heels, and her hair was pulled back into a low bun. Some wild tendrils fought to get loose—the hairstylist had given up trying to tame them. Her make-up was minimal, yet effective.

She was wearing a string of pearls around her neck and simple pearl drop earrings. A matching bracelet. The diamond stud high in her ear twinkled at her. She had a rebellious urge to leave it there and see how Aristedes would react. But the fact that Maddi wanted to provoke him made her take it out quickly, placing it onto a little tray.

When Laia had noticed her numerous ear piercings, she'd given the stud to Maddi, saying, 'I always wanted to have loads of piercings, but I wasn't allowed. Wear this for me and I'll get to enjoy it through you.'

So that was why it was special to her. It was one half of a pair owned by Laia.

She hadn't expected Aristedes to be so incensed by a fairly conservative piercing, but when he'd asked her earlier if a lover had given it to her he'd looked as if he might explode.

It really shouldn't be attractive to her that he was so incensed by a tiny piece of jewellery, but Maddi found that it only made her want to push him more. To see him react. He was so cool. So sure. It was intoxicating to know she had the ability to affect him—even if it was just by irritating him.

Because irritating him was preferable to thinking about the fact that she was about to go out in front of people and be seen as a princess. Something she wasn't ready for—not even when she was pretending to be Laia. A persona she could hide behind.

'Princess Laia? The King is ready for you.'

Maddi's insides plummeted with fear, but she turned around and forced a smile for Hannah. It wasn't as if she had any reason to *really* care about this event, but she found that she was caring about making a good impression.

On Aristedes, whispered a sly voice.

As Maddi followed Hannah to meet the King, on wobbly legs she had to admit that, yes, she had a massively inconvenient crush on the guy—but she had to remember where her loyalties lay. With her sister. She wasn't here for herself.

As the King had pointed out so brutally earlier. *'If*

you were Princess Laia...but you're not.' That had stung far more than it should. But it was a necessary reminder. She was here under sufferance only, for as long as it took to ensure Laia got her freedom.

CHAPTER FIVE

'THIS IS FOR YOU.'

Maddi looked down at the small velvet box in the King's palm. She looked back up at him, nonplussed. He emitted a sound like a frustrated sigh and opened the box, revealing a ring.

Maddi couldn't help a small gasp. It was beautiful. A large round diamond, surrounded by smaller round emeralds in a gold setting, with more diamonds forming a V shape on either side of the centrepiece before tapering into a gold band.

It was intricate and it looked like an antique. She asked, 'How old is it?'

'It's been passed down from bride to bride in my family for generations.'

Maddi dragged her gaze up. 'But I can't wear this. What if I lose it?'

'You have to wear it. It's the ring people will be expecting Princess Laia to wear. If it's not on your finger, people will talk.'

The King put down the box and took Maddi's hand. She wanted to pull away. Not just because of her reaction to his touch, but because suddenly this was becoming very…real.

The ring was heavy and, amazingly, it fitted. Almost like a mockery of what she and Laia were doing. As if they were doomed no matter what they did.

She shivered a little.

'Cold?'

Maddi shook her head.

Aristedes said, 'Good, then let's go.'

Ari was ultra-conscious of the woman at his side. And for all the wrong reasons. She was dressed perfectly appropriately—exactly like a crown princess, elegant and sophisticated. But he felt the energy emanating from her—unpredictable and electric.

He realised, as they stood and greeted people, that she might very well do something to subvert the marriage pact, even though he thought he'd convinced her that it would be bad for Princess Laia and Isla'Rosa to do anything rash.

It was for that reason, he told himself, that he kept a hand on her elbow—so that he could move quickly if she dared to say anything out of turn. But after a moment he realised that she was trembling lightly. He slanted a look down at her and realised she looked like a deer in the headlights. Terrified.

He said something to his chief aide and suddenly the line of people waiting to greet them was diverted discreetly, leaving them alone for a moment. He turned Maddi to face him. She looked up, still wide-eyed.

'What's wrong?' he asked.

'What's wrong?' she squeaked. 'What's wrong is that I've never done this before and I shouldn't be here.'

Anger and irritation made him stern. 'And yet here you are—precisely because that's how you have engineered it.'

His conscience pricked. He took situations like this completely for granted. He'd been facing them since before he'd hit double digits. He could sleepwalk his way through a meet-and-greet and no one would even know. He might get some satisfaction out of Maddi squirming, but it wasn't going to do him any favours if she didn't at least look comfortable.

'Just let me do all the talking. No one expects you to say anything. Just smile. But keep your mouth closed so the gap in your teeth isn't so obvious.'

A spark came into her eyes. 'I'm surprised you haven't insisted on dental surgery to correct it.'

Ari was surprised to feel a rush of negativity at that suggestion. 'Don't be ridiculous.'

He was aware of the crowd around them, eyes all over them. He acted on impulse. He took Maddi's hand, the one on which she wore the engagement ring. He lifted it to his mouth and pressed his lips against the back of her hand, keeping his eyes on hers.

Flashes went off around them as the press pack seized their photo opportunity.

It was an old-fashioned, chaste gesture, but even as he made the move entirely cynically, Ari's nostrils were filled with Maddi's scent…light, floral tones with something more complicated underneath.

He saw how her hazel eyes flared, amber and golden. The way colour stained her cheeks. Then she bit her lip.

By the time Ari had lifted his mouth from her hand he was on fire all over, and had an urge to wrap his free arm around her, haul her into him and press his mouth against hers in a very public display of desire. Not his usual style at all.

But something about her made him feral, a reversion into some sort of man guided by base instincts and lusts.

This is why she's dangerous.

She wouldn't have to say a word. She'd cause carnage just by fusing his brain cells into a heat haze.

With an effort he really didn't appreciate, he took her hand and tucked it into the crook of his elbow, and then turned back to face the room.

At a discreet nod of his head, his aides let the guests approach again.

After what felt like hours, Maddi's cheeks and feet were aching. And her hand felt as if all the small bones in it had been crushed by the countless firm handshakes.

The King must have seen her cradle her hand, because he said wryly, 'You'll learn not to let them take your whole hand.'

Maddi huffed. 'You could have given me a heads-up.'

They were standing by the wall of the terrace, with the sea far below. Dusk was starting to stain the sky with lavender hues. Maddi hated to admit it, but she did feel a little mesmerised by the beauty of the place. And its scents…the smell of wild flowers and the salty tang of the sea.

Guards stood nearby—a merciful buffer between them and the now dwindling crowd.

She felt Aristedes's gaze on her and looked at him.

He arched a brow. Fair enough, she supposed, considering everything she'd put him through.

Then he said, 'It was a success.'

Maddi tried not to notice how tall and broad he was. He really was stupendously gorgeous. He'd been impressively indefatigable all afternoon. She felt as wrung out as a dishcloth.

'It was? I barely said a word.'

'Everyone saw you and believed what they thought they saw. Princess Laia. That's all we needed.'

'What if we meet someone who really knows her, though?'

The King must have made a gesture, because a waiter materialised with a tray holding two flutes of sparkling wine. Aristedes passed Maddi a glass. She took a big sip, relishing the sensation of relaxing her face muscles. She wished she could slip off her shoes.

'One thing in our favour is that there isn't much traffic between Santanger and Isla'Rosa because of the centuries of conflict. Hence the marriage pact—to encourage peace and unity between the two nations.'

Maddi took another gulp of wine to avoid meeting his eye. She had to admit that, in spite of Laia's feelings, she could understand the benefit in promoting peace. But she was with her sister in not wanting Isla'Rosa to be consumed by the much bigger and richer Santanger.

The wine was making her feel a little reckless, so Maddi said, 'Have you thought about who you'll marry after you've acknowledged that this marriage pact is all but null and void?'

King Aristedes went still. He'd been looking out to the sea. His gaze swivelled to her. 'This marriage pact is not "null and void". Princess Laia was born to a life of duty—just like me. In the end she will do what is right. She is merely behaving like a petulant teenager who knows that ultimately she has no choice. The sooner she realises this, the sooner this tedious game will be over.'

Maddi shook her head. 'But it's an archaic agreement. Surely there are more modern ways to foster peace? She couldn't be making it more obvious that she doesn't want to marry you.'

The King's jaw clenched. Maddi realised then that he probably wasn't used to people speaking so plainly to him. But she had nothing to lose here. And it felt a little exhilarating.

He said tersely, 'I was told at the age of eight that I would marry Princess Laia.'

Maddi held in a gasp. 'But she would have only been a baby.'

'Just born.'

She couldn't help but see an image of a small, serious child, trying to understand such a monumental thing. It made her heart clench.

'That's a lot to put on an eight-year-old's shoulders. Never mind a baby's.'

'Nevertheless, this is how marriages between royal families have happened for generations. It's what we expect.'

'And how many happy royal families do you know?' Maddi asked.

Aristedes's face tightened. 'That's not the point. The point is—'

Maddi put up her hand. 'Duty, responsibility, stability... I get it.'

A discreet cough sounded from nearby.

Maddi flushed at the King's warning look.

He looked over her head. 'Yes, Santo?'

'Sorry to interrupt, Your Majesty, but the call you were waiting for is on hold.'

'Thank you. I'll take it on my phone.' He put a hand into his jacket's inside pocket and took out a sleek mobile phone. He looked at Maddi expressionlessly. 'That is all. Santo will escort you back to your suite.'

His cursory dismissal filled Maddi with conflicting emotions. Chief of which, though she hated to admit it, was *hurt*. He obviously hadn't appreciated their exchange. Hadn't appreciated her opinion. It reminded her that she wasn't of this world. That she'd been rejected by it long ago.

Not for the first time the difference between her and her sister couldn't be starker. On her birth, Laia had already been promised in marriage to a future king. On Maddi's birth, she'd been born to a single unwed mother, heartbroken and abandoned, promised to no one.

If anything, this event had just demonstrated how out of her depth she was. And how far removed she was from being a princess.

She hated the feeling of insecurity that washed over her. Worse, the feeling of rejection.

Before Aristedes turned away she said, in a low voice, 'Is this how you'd be treating Princess Laia? Wheeling her out for viewings and then shutting her away again? Making no attempt to get to know her?'

'If Princess Laia was here, you can rest assured I would, of course, be making an effort to get to know her—after all, she will be my wife. But you are not her, and after Laia and I are married, you and I will never meet again.'

So why would I bother with you?

He didn't have to say it. The words hung in the air.

Aristedes turned and walked away to a quiet corner of the garden and took his call.

Maddi felt stunned. Well, she'd asked for that. She suddenly saw the ruthlessness that had been hiding in plain sight underneath his very suave exterior and it sent a shiver down her spine. *This* man would indeed track Princess Laia down and bring her back here to do her duty, of that she had no doubt.

And in the meantime, she was just an irritating inconvenience.

Somehow, in the last couple of days, Maddi had been fostering some kind of notion that he might not *like* her, or this situation, but that he was…intrigued by her. And that he too felt the electric charge between them. That…

What? asked a snarky voice in her head. *That he's become more interested in getting to know you than the woman who is destined to be the mother of his children? The next Queen of Santanger?*

Full of swirling emotions that she'd stirred up all by herself, by provoking the King into telling her exactly how inconsequential she was, Maddi started when someone coughed discreetly behind her. She turned around to see Santo, the aide, still waiting.

He put out his hand, 'If you'll follow me, please?'

Maddi blindly followed him on wooden legs, feeling ridiculously vulnerable for the first time since she'd taken the audacious move to do something drastic to save her sister.

She'd become adept at not allowing the rejection by her father to get to her, but sometimes it crept through the defences she'd built up over the years and reminded her that she had a hole inside her, and no matter how much she might try to tell herself it didn't matter, *it did*. And the fact that she'd just allowed King Aristedes to remind her of how painful this wound could be was not welcome.

How was it that a man she'd met only days ago could have such a terrifying effect on her emotions?

There was a knock on the door, and then, 'Sorry to disturb—'

'What is it?' Ari snapped moodily. And then felt immediate contrition when he turned from the window and saw the wide eyes of one of his longest-serving aides at the door.

This wasn't like him. He strove at all times to be the opposite of his father, who had been mercurial and unpredictable.

Thanks to his father's disregard for his wife, and his love of other women, Ari had learnt at an early age to depend on himself. He'd received no benevolent guiding hand from either parent. Neither had his brother. He'd had to learn from aides and watching his parents to know how *not* to be.

He'd always treated his lovers with respect. He'd never cheated. And Dax was the same, even if the tabloids made it look otherwise. And yet here he was, distracted and thinking of…a woman. Who wasn't even the woman he was due to marry.

Irritation prickled again. He forced it down.

His aide was still in the doorway, looking nervous. Ari said, 'I'm sorry. My mind was…elsewhere.'

On Maddi, and the way she'd looked after he'd dismissed her the evening before.

He cursed silently.

'I just wanted to remind you that you are taking Princess Laia out for lunch today and it's almost time to leave.'

He'd forgotten his own schedule. Again, that was not like him. He was fastidious about his schedule and his plans. And he never let anyone down. Not even his imposter fiancée.

'Is she waiting for me?'

'Yes, sir. Down by the main courtyard.'

His aide left. In spite of his best efforts, Ari felt his blood heat with anticipation. But the last words he'd said to her yesterday still reverberated in his head, sickeningly…

'But you are not her, and after Laia and I are married, you and I will never meet again.'

He'd been rude. And she'd looked hurt. Not what he would have expected of the woman who'd had the gall to impersonate the Crown Princess of Isla'Rosa. But if he was being brutally honest he knew that his rudeness had stemmed from how she made him feel, how she pushed his buttons with such ease.

She had a way of saying things, asking questions, that seemed to undermine every belief he'd taken for granted his whole life. And he didn't welcome that. His route had been mapped out for a long time, and he'd been perfectly content to follow it. Especially when it promised smooth waters and no drama. But from the moment this woman had impersonated his fiancée those waters had become choppy and much murkier.

Ari felt defensive. Some might forgive him for being rude, considering where they were and what was happening. Princess Laia and his brother were AWOL. God only knew where. And he was being forced to act out a charade with this…this doppelganger, who just had to breathe beside him to make his blood boil over with irritation and lust.

He didn't have to woo this woman. She was a complete stranger.

Is she, though? asked a little voice. *Why does she feel so familiar, then, and yet mysterious? Why is she so easy to talk to?*

Ari scowled at himself as he pulled on his jacket. Maddi Smith was an interloper. She'd tricked him. But he had to concede that if she *had* actually been Princess Laia, then he would be wooing her. Even though their marriage was a sure thing, he would obviously want her to feel as desired and accepted as possible.

And, following that logic, he would have to treat Maddi the same and not let her get to him. If anyone sensed the tension between them it would cause whispers, and that was the last thing they needed.

He needed her to promote a picture of happy unity— because he had total faith in his brother reappearing with Princess Laia and no doubt he would be marrying the right woman in a couple of weeks.

The fact that Maddi was the first woman he'd ever

met who had managed to get under his skin so comprehensively was a mere irritation en route to the start of this next phase of his life with his Queen at his side.

Maddi was down on her hands and knees, desperately searching for a small pearl drop earring. One minute it had been in her ear and the next it had fallen to the stone floor, here in the main central courtyard.

Hannah was on her hands and knees too, saying anxiously, 'I'm sure we'll find it, Princess Laia, please don't ruin your clothes!'

The bodyguards were hunting as well, using their phone torches to try and see into the cracks between the flagstones.

There was a distinct cough from somewhere far above their heads and Maddi's stomach sank. Not that it could sink much more from her inelegant position so close to the ground.

She lifted her head and came eye to eye with a pair of very sleek shoes. They led up to a pair of navy trousers, encasing very long legs, a slim waist…white shirt and matching navy jacket.

King Aristedes. She stood up, brushing dust from her black jumpsuit. She'd felt so sophisticated just moments before, but now she could feel her hair coming loose from its low bun and her face was hot.

He arched a brow in question and Maddi burned inwardly with humiliation, remembering his dismissive and cutting words from yesterday. She'd told herself that nothing he said should matter, and she'd thought she'd convinced herself she could stay immune, but within one second of seeing him again she felt as vulnerable as she had yesterday.

At that moment she really didn't like him.

'I've lost an earring.' She touched her ear.

He frowned. 'It's just an earring.'

'It's a pearl earring, and presumably very expensive.'

Hannah had moved away discreetly, to keep looking, but was no longer on her hands and knees.

The King was impatient, and he put out his hand. 'It's replaceable. Don't worry about it.'

But Maddi hadn't been brought up not to care about valuable items. She knew their worth because her mother had had to work for everything, in spite of the maintenance she'd received from the King of Isla'Rosa.

Stubbornly, she didn't move, and looked down at the ground again. And there, as if to help her out, she saw something white winking at her between two stones.

She let out a triumphant sound and bent down to pick it up, holding it aloft. 'See? Found it.'

She grinned and put it back in her ear. The King's gaze went to her mouth and stopped there. Maddi shut it abruptly, aware of what he'd told her about hiding the gap in her teeth.

His face darkened and he said curtly, 'Can we go, now that the mystery of the lost earring has been solved?'

He led the way out of the courtyard to where a sleek SUV was waiting. Maddi was sorely tempted to stick her tongue out at his back, but she resisted the childish urge.

Once in the back of the SUV, driving out of the palace grounds and down the mountain towards the city of Santanger, Maddi couldn't help saying, 'Apart from this situation, which you're obviously not happy with, are you usually so grumpy?'

Aristedes's jaw clenched. He pressed a button and the privacy divider went up between them and the driver.

Maddi was genuinely contrite. 'Sorry, I forgot.'

He looked at her, stern. 'What on earth were you doing, on your hands and knees, scrabbling around in the dirt?'

'I told you—looking for the earring. I know it must be valuable.'

He looked nonplussed. 'It's just jewellery.'

She lifted the hand where the engagement ring sat snugly—too snugly—on her finger. 'Like this is *just jewellery?*'

He made a face. 'That's different, of course.'

'So, are you? Always this grumpy?'

And rude, she might have added, if she'd had the nerve.

Something in his demeanour changed for a second, and there was the ghost of a twitch in his lips. So fleeting that Maddi might have imagined it, but it set her heart racing.

'No,' he replied dryly. 'It's uniquely your effect on me.'

For a moment something shimmered between them. Light and delicate. Then Aristedes's phone rang from his pocket and he plucked it out, saying, 'Excuse me. I need to take this.'

He spoke rapidly, in the local dialect, a mix of Spanish and Italian. Much like the language on Isla'Rosa.

Maddi had been doing her best to learn it, but she couldn't keep up with the King's rapid-fire delivery.

The SUV was now driving slowly through the charming streets of the city and winding its way up another hill, where it came to a stop. The bodyguard in the front passenger seat got out and opened Maddi's door. She stepped out and realised they were on the top of a hill that overlooked the city and the sea beyond. The views were spectacular.

They walked around a corner and Maddi stopped in her tracks. A restaurant was perched precipitously on the hillside. It was made of glass and wood, on several levels, with massive windows and an outdoor terrace. It was an astounding work of architecture and design. Even she could see that, with no real knowledge of such things.

Aristedes put a hand lightly at her elbow to guide her into the building where the manager waited. He was holding the door open and bowed profusely as they approached. 'Your Majesty... Princess Laia, welcome to Paradiso.'

Even Maddi could translate that. Paradise. And it was. They were led to a table tucked discreetly to one side of the upper level, with floor-to-ceiling windows showcasing the amazing view.

When they were sitting down, Maddi couldn't help saying, 'I don't think I've ever been to a more impressive restaurant.'

'And you haven't even tasted the food yet. The best the Mediterranean has to offer.'

Maddi risked a glance at Aristedes, who was the picture of casual elegance even as he exuded a masculine edge that was a reminder of the latent power sheathed in respectable clothes.

'I presume this is an exercise in our being seen and promoting the myth that we're getting to know one another?'

Even though he would obviously prefer to be elsewhere. With his real princess.

'That's exactly what this is.'

He popped an olive into his mouth.

Maddi had been aware of discreet looks from the other patrons as they'd been escorted through the restaurant. It was obviously far too elegant a place for people to rubberneck.

'Do you resent having to do this with me?' she asked, and then cursed herself for looking for punishment. Had she not learnt that lesson yesterday?

The King looked at her, and she felt pinned by that dark gaze. It reminded her of how it had felt when his mouth had touched her hand the day before.

A waiter appeared with dips and different breads.

Aristedes said, 'I took the liberty of ordering for you, presuming that you'll enjoy most of what's on the menu.'

Maddi was about to protest that she might have liked to choose for herself, but who was she kidding? 'Thank you. I'll be interested to see what you think I'll like.'

The dips and bread were all delicious, and full of flavour. Her favourite was the tomato bread with pesto sauce.

'Try the wine.'

Maddi took a sip of red wine and closed her eyes. It tasted of sun-warmed grapes and blackcurrant. She opened her eyes again to find Aristedes staring at her.

She blushed. 'Sorry, I get a little carried away.'

'Maybe you should have been a chef?'

Maddi wiped her mouth. 'I worked as a commis chef in a restaurant in Dublin once, and after seeing the pressure chefs are under, it didn't appeal. I prefer a much less pressured environment. Like cooking for friends.'

Or her sister, who had been ridiculously impressed with Maddi's pretty basic skills.

'Why did you and your mother leave Isla'Rosa?'

Aristedes had slipped the question in before Maddi could really give herself time to consider it. Wonder what telling him might reveal.

Carefully, she said, 'We left because her relationship with my father broke down. He didn't want to be with us.'

Maddi said the words with a clipped voice, hoping Aristedes wouldn't hear the emotion behind them.

'That must have been hard...to leave her home and move across Europe.'

'To a much wetter country.' She shrugged, belying the lingering hurt for her mother's pain. 'I was a baby. I didn't know any better.'

'I've been to Ireland...it's beautiful.'

Maddi looked at him. 'You have?' She couldn't recall any state visits from the King—she was sure she would have remembered.

He nodded. 'They were under the radar, not official. Usually to attend financial conferences. The President has extended to me an open invitation for a state visit. Maybe I'll go some day...with my Queen.'

For some reason, the thought of King Aristedes visiting Ireland with Laia at his side pricked Maddi painfully.

She forced a smile. 'You should go at the earliest opportunity. The hospitality is second to none.'

Their main courses were delivered—delicate parcels of pasta filled with ricotta cheese in a light sauce. They ate in a surprisingly companionable silence, but once the plates were cleared Aristedes said, 'I need to apologise.'

She was surprised. 'You need to apologise to me? Shouldn't I be apologising to you every day, because I'm here and you're trying to track down Princess Laia?'

His face darkened and she regretted opening her mouth. She always said too much.

'Sorry, please, go on.'

'Yesterday…what I said to you was not necessary and it was rude. You are obviously close to Princess Laia— close enough to carry out this stunt on her behalf—'

'It was my idea,' Maddi blurted out, even as she registered a soothing of the hurt he'd caused yesterday.

Aristedes stopped. 'What?'

She nodded, hating it that he was now going to retract his apology. But she couldn't let him believe this had been Laia's doing.

'I told her to run. I told her I would try and pass myself off as her.'

There was a taut moment of silence, and then he said, 'She had her chance to do the right thing, but she did as you suggested. She made her choice. This doesn't change anything, really. Except maybe to demonstrate that you're not entirely without integrity.'

A waiter brought coffee and small pastries.

Aristedes went on. 'As I was saying, you're obviously close to Princess Laia, and she trusts you. She will undoubtedly choose to retain you as her lady-in-waiting once she is Queen here, and that will be her choice, of course.'

Maddi was filled with so many conflicting thoughts that she felt a little dizzy. His apology was a surprise, and mollified her somewhat. His arrogant assumption that in spite of all evidence to the contrary Laia would still agree to be his wife was enraging. But worse than all that, and most exposing, was the way she felt to hear him declare so magnanimously that she could remain as Laia's lady-in-waiting. That he would be happy to see her every day and tolerate her presence, even though this…this current of awareness throbbed between them.

And that was when Maddi had to realise that she was being a prize idiot. Because all this awareness was obviously only on her side. This man looked at her and saw nothing but a nuisance. An obstacle between him and his Queen.

She had developed a crush on him on sight, but the only thing she aroused in him was serious irritation. He'd been pretending there was something between them to mock her.

And one thing she knew already. It would be intolerable to be in close proximity to this man every day and not be *his*.

The strength of that conviction shook Maddi.

How much he affected her!

She put down her napkin. 'I'm feeling a little light-headed, actually. Would you mind if we went back to the palace?'

CHAPTER SIX

ARI LOOKED AT Maddi across the back of the vehicle as they drove up the mountain towards the palace. She looked pale. He knew he shouldn't be feeling concerned. This woman had severely disrupted his life. And yet he couldn't help wondering if he'd said something...

Maybe it was throwing her into the deep end of Princess Laia's schedule that was overwhelming her...and it would be just punishment if it was. Except right now Ari didn't have any appetite for revenge or punishment.

What he felt was much more ambiguous. And beneath that was the ever-present thrum of desire.

Her arms were bare in the jumpsuit, and they looked slim, but strong. Her waist was encircled with a gold belt. The jewellery—those pearl earrings—were the essence of understated glamour. Perfect for a queen-to-be. Except he found himself looking for that diamond stud she'd worn high in her ear, like some sort of...free spirit.

But he'd told her to take it out...like a censorious parent. Was that who he was now? Staid and conservative? Stern?

'Are you okay?' he asked.

Maddi nodded and glanced at him. 'I'm fine... I just...needed a little air, maybe.'

She did have some more colour in her cheeks now, and Ari felt something in him relaxing. On an impulse he said, 'I was going to go to my stables and check the horses, maybe go for a ride. Would you be interested?'

She turned to him, eyes wide. More hair had fallen loose from the bun, as if it was impossible to contain her hair fully. 'I'd love to.' She made a face. 'But I only started learning to ride this year on Isla'Rosa, so I'm not very good.'

'That's not a problem. We'll give you one of the more sedate horses.'

'That would be amazing.'

She smiled, and it took Ari's breath away for a second. This woman was full of something he'd never really encountered. Her emotions rose up and she appeared to have no filter for hiding them. They burst out of her irrepressibly. She hadn't been calcified, like him and everyone he knew. It disarmed him.

He instructed the driver to take them straight to the stables and put in a call to have Hannah bring some clothes for Maddi.

Maddi was glad to be engaging in something active to take her mind off how Aristedes made her feel and the things he said that cut her when they shouldn't.

They'd arrived at the stables and Hannah had been waiting there with more suitable clothes. Maddi had changed in a room used by the grooms, and now wore khaki jodhpurs and a white short-sleeved polo top and black boots. And a hard hat on her head. .

She'd given Hannah all the jewellery and was glad to feel a little less encumbered. She'd pulled her hair out of the bun and into a low ponytail. For the first time in days she felt more like herself again.

It was her sister who had taken her horse riding for the first time. Laia was a proficient horsewoman, having learnt from an early age. And Maddi loved it, even if the horses still terrified her a little, with their size and sheer power.

There was a knock at the door. 'Princess Laia? The King is ready.'

And she shouldn't keep the King waiting. Maddi almost rolled her eyes. But secretly she was excited to see him in a far less structured habitat. She could already imagine him on a horse...the effortless grace and athleticism.

When she did emerge into the yard she couldn't see him. All she saw was the back of a very tall man tending to a massive chestnut horse. He was wearing faded jeans that clung to his muscular backside and strong thighs with such explicitness that Maddi couldn't look away.

For a moment she felt a giddy sense of relief—the King hadn't had a unique effect on her after all—but then he turned around and Maddi's skin goosebumped all over.

It was the King.

Of course it was.

He was wearing a polo shirt, like her, short-sleeved, showing off impressive biceps. His olive skin was gleaming.

She walked over and he stood aside, his gaze sweeping over her. She felt warm, and tried to ignore this one-sided mortifying awareness.

The horse was saddled and ready. He patted its neck. 'Here she is—La Reina.'

Maddi squinted at him. 'Is that meant to be a joke? She's called The Queen?'

He shook his head. 'Not at all. She *is* the Queen here. She's eighteen years old and she's the dam of some of the best racehorses in Europe today. Some even in Ireland.'

Maddi came closer, nervously. 'She was a racehorse?'

'Very successful, yes. My father bought her as a yearling at a sale in Dublin, when Dax and I were younger.'

Maddi reached out and tentatively touched this great dam's back. 'So you've had her for ever?'

'Yes, I guess so.'

'Is this a stud?'

'No. We do have training grounds and a separate stud nearby, but this is just the palace stables, where we keep La Reina and other horses we use purely for riding. Her mating days are long over now—aren't they, my beauty?'

Maddi watched the King's big, graceful hand and long fingers running over the horse's neck. She whinnied softly and Maddi could empathise.

The nearest stirrup was low and Aristedes said, 'You know how to mount a horse?'

Maddi balked. 'You want me to ride her? What if I hurt her or something?'

He smiled, and for a moment Maddi couldn't think. He looked completely different when he smiled. Younger. Carefree. Less stern.

'You can't hurt her. She's survived more than a novice rider, believe me.'

Maddi stood as Laia had taught her, by the neck of the horse, and took the reins in her hand. Then she lifted her left foot into the stirrup. Absurdly conscious of Aristedes behind her, she put her other hand on the saddle and somehow managed to mount the horse without making a complete fool of herself.

He stood at her foot and adjusted the stirrup, bringing it up higher. He looked at her. 'Not bad. You have a good posture in the saddle. You know the basics?'

Maddi was not a little terrified. La Reina was a big horse and she felt very high up. She nodded, but said, 'The very basic basics.'

'Just relax and get a feel for the horse underneath you. She'll guide you.'

A groom led another horse into the yard and Maddi gulped. This horse was a massive gleaming black stallion. He made La Reina look almost petite. Aristedes went over and adjusted the reins before mounting the horse in one effortless muscular movement.

Maddi fidgeted on the horse, to ease the sudden sensation between her legs. The horse moved under her. She stopped, suddenly terrified. Laia had only let her practise on the smallest and most sedate horses at the castle on Isla'Rosa.

Aristedes was securing his hat on his head. He looked back. 'Okay?'

Maddi was nervous. 'We're going to go slowly, yes?'

He nudged his horse with his knee and they started walking out of the yard. 'Very slowly...don't worry. La Reina will follow me and Sooty automatically.'

Maddi nearly fell off her horse. 'Sooty?'

Surely that name was an affront to the majestic beast in front of her?

Aristedes waited for her to come alongside him and then both horses went side by side out onto a wide track.

'Dax and I got this horse when we were teenagers. Typically Dax didn't want to share, so we had to fight for him.'

'What did you do?'

'We had a fist fight. First one down loses.'

Maddi winced. 'I bet your mother was delighted.'

He made a face. 'Yeah, not so much… I broke Dax's nose.' Aristedes looked at her. 'Suffice it to say it was the last fist fight we had.'

'But… Sooty? I'm sorry, but that's almost an insult. Surely he should be called Caesar or Nero or… anything else?'

'As revenge for me winning, Dax logged his name in the official system before I could. And so here is Sooty.'

Maddi couldn't keep the laughter down. It came bubbling out and she had to throw her head back. She could just imagine a young Aristedes's appalled expression.

'I'm glad you find it amusing.'

'Sorry,' she spluttered, getting control of herself, 'That's just too…evil of Dax.'

After a couple of minutes of companionable silence Maddi found she was getting used to La Reina. She bent down and patted her neck, silently thanking her for not throwing her off as soon as she'd landed on her back.

She sneaked a look at Aristedes in the saddle and almost wept at how beautiful he was. He held the reins easily in one hand, his other resting on his thigh. His body's motion with the horse was perfectly in sync. Maddi felt as if she was bouncing all over the place, but she tried to mimic his posture and discovered an easier rhythm.

The trail was getting narrower, and Maddi was glad she didn't have to try and steer La Reina. The horse seemed happy to just follow Aristedes and Sooty.

Then Maddi spied a beach down below, wide and golden. Unusual... Most of the beaches on Isla'Rosa were stony, so she'd assumed Santanger would be the same.

They made their way down the trail, with scents of herbs and flowers and earth permeating the air around them. It was just the right temperature. Warm. The sun not too fierce.

At last they were on a level with the beach and it opened out before them, wide and pristine.

Maddi lifted a hand to shade her eyes. 'Wow, it's so quiet here. I would have expected it to be thronged.'

'We're still on palace property.'

Of course. Maddi should have realised.

Sooty was dancing under Aristedes and he said, 'I need to give him his head—will you be okay if I give him a gallop?'

Maddi waved a hand. 'We'll be fine. You go ahead.'

So she could watch him like a proper voyeur.

And they were magnificent, man and beast. They trotted down to the water's edge and then they were off, galloping through the sea foam. A vision in masculine beauty, muscles rippling, Aristedes was in total control, barely moving in the saddle.

La Reina seemed content to meander up and down

near the treeline, but suddenly out of nowhere a bird was startled and rose out of a bush, squawking loudly. Before Maddi could do anything the horse had reared up.

Somehow, miraculously, she managed to cling on. But then the horse bolted. Maddi realised she had absolutely no control over this powerful beast, which suddenly didn't feel like such a sedate grand dam any more. She felt like a bullet.

Every bone in Maddi's body was rattling as she clung on to the reins for dear life. Surely she'd come to a stop at some point? But they were heading straight for a clump of jagged rocks at the other end of the beach and the horse showed no signs of slowing.

Maddi was about to close her eyes and pray for mercy when a streak of black appeared beside her. Aristedes leant out of his saddle to grab Maddi's reins and he managed to bring both horses to a canter, and then a trot, and eventually to a walk, mere feet away from the rocks—one of which was particularly spiky.

Maddi barely had a chance to get her breath back before hands were reaching for her, around her waist, and she was off the horse and standing on legs that shook like jelly.

Aristedes took off her hat, threw it aside. His was gone too. 'Are you hurt? Are you okay?'

She couldn't answer because he was running his hands all over her—arms, waist, hips—and crouching down to check her legs. He stood up and she realised she was clutching at his arms and her teeth were chattering.

He cursed and pulled her into him, rubbing his hands up and down her back. 'I'm sorry, that was my fault. I should never have left you alone. La Reina is still powerful. Something must have startled her.'

Maddi pulled back. She was feeling marginally less wobbly, and now other sensations were piercing the shock and adrenaline rush. Like how close she was to Aristedes, their bodies pressed together. How his touch was tender and comforting, but also like an electric charge, transmitting something much more potent than comfort or tenderness.

There were still tremors running through her body but her teeth had stopped chattering. She tried to speak. 'It was a bird… I think. Flew out of a…bush.'

Aristedes looked down at her. 'She could have thrown you.'

Maddi tried to smile but her mouth wouldn't work. 'She tried.'

'Maddi, I'm sorry. The last thing you need when you're learning how to ride is a scare like that. It can put people off for life.'

Maddi didn't want to seem weak or scared. Stoutly, she said, 'I'm okay. I can get back on.' She mentally crossed her fingers, hoping she wouldn't suddenly be terrified.

Aristedes's mouth twitched. 'We'll leave it a minute, hmm?'

Something shifted in the air between them. An awareness of their bodies so close together. Of Maddi's breasts crushed against Aristedes's broad and very hard chest.

They were hip to hip. Thigh to thigh. Suddenly certain that she wouldn't be able to hide her reaction behind shock any more, Maddi tried to pull back—but his arms didn't budge.

'Where are you going?'

She looked up and swallowed. His dark gaze was intense. Surely not… She wanted to shake her head.

She said, 'To stand on my own two feet?'

'Overrated.'

Maddi's brain went into a spin. Aristedes caught some of her hair around his hand. Of course it had fallen loose. It was untameable. Maddi wanted to groan. She must look as if she'd been pulled through a bush backwards.

Then he said, almost musingly, 'I should have known you weren't Laia the moment I laid eyes on you…'

'Why?'

'Because she never made me want to look twice. She never made me *want*.'

Maddi's legs nearly buckled again. She locked her knees. She was wondering if she was dreaming. But Aristedes was looking at her mouth now…hungrily. It was a hunger that caught fire inside her, deep down. She didn't know why, but she'd always had an instinct that this fire could exist. Stubbornly, she'd hoped that it did, and now she was being consumed by it.

She whispered, 'I thought it was just me.'

He shook his head. 'You make me crazy.'

Maddi ducked her head. 'I know. Because of—'

But her chin was tipped back before she could complete her sentence and Aristedes was shaking his head again.

'Because of *this*.'

And then, before Maddi could take another breath, he

was kissing her. She was suspended in time and place for a second, as his strong, firm mouth moved over hers, and then, as if coming out of a trance, she was suddenly kissing him back with a ferocity that might have scared her if she'd had a functioning brain cell left in her head.

Waves of relief washed through her.

He wanted her too.

And then there were much more potent things.

Desire fast turning to lust.

He angled her head and she opened her mouth on a breath. Everything changed. His tongue touched hers and Maddi's heart pounded at the electric shock it brought, sending a jolt through her entire body, down to between her legs, where she *ached*.

He was demanding a response from her that she willingly gave. Matching him stroke for stroke. She was intoxicated.

He clamped his hands on her waist and pulled her even closer. She gasped into his mouth when she felt the hard evidence of his arousal against her lower body.

But even in the midst of this moment of total and utter conflagration, Maddi had the very unsettling sense of something else. She felt as if she was...*coming home*.

But she couldn't unpick that now. It was too confusing. Disturbing...

Aristedes broke the kiss.

Maddi was gasping, dizzy. She opened her eyes with an effort and for a second he was a blur. Then he came back into focus. His face was stark with the hunger she felt. Eyes burning.

Her mouth was swollen.

He looked at her and shook his head. 'Who *are* you?'

Maddi couldn't speak. She knew he wasn't just asking her to repeat her name. She could have asked the same of him. Right now, he didn't remotely resemble the man that Laia had always described as uptight, strict, humourless.

This man was the most exciting person Maddi had ever met, and just moments ago he'd touched her with a tenderness that she'd never encountered before. Not even from her own mother.

One of the hands on her waist moved up, disturbingly close to the underside of her breast. Maddi's breath grew choppy again.

He said, 'I've been dreaming of you... Of touching you.'

Between her legs she felt hot and damp. 'You have?'

He nodded. His hand crept under her top. She could feel the roughness of his palms and almost groaned. He was a king...he should have soft hands from being waited on. But he didn't. He had the hands of a worker.

And then one hand was cupping the weight of her breast.

Maddi bit her lip and Aristedes tugged it free with his thumb. He bent his head and kissed her again. This time slowly, carefully, thoroughly. He squeezed the generous flesh of her breast and she moaned into his mouth, pressing closer, relishing the hard evidence of his desire.

His hand on her breast squeezed harder. Maddi's nipples were stiff, tingling. Aching. And then his thumb found the hard tip and teased it, over and over, through the flimsy covering of lace. Maddi was turning into a boneless pool of lust. She didn't feel human any more. She'd become a creature of base needs.

Aristedes broke the kiss again, breathing harshly. 'I could take you right here and now…'

Maddi opened her eyes. She should be shocked by what he was suggesting. But the fact was that every cell in her body vibrated with agreement.

Yes, please. Take me right now.

But Aristedes pulled back, and Maddi had to stop a sound leaving her mouth. A sound of distress.

He took his hand from her breast. Pulled her top down again. 'This isn't the time or place.'

Maddi tried desperately to remember why it wasn't a good idea to throw caution to the wind.

A series of unwelcome answers flooded her brain:

Because he's the King…because he hates you…because you're a virgin…

She went still. Pulled back too. She felt wobbly without his hands on her.

He reached for her again. 'Are you okay?'

But she put a hand up. She'd just revealed *everything*. 'I'm fine.'

She looked around, as if seeing the beach for the first time. Had the earth shifted on its axis? It felt like it.

'We should get back to the palace. My security team will be wondering where we are.'

He emitted a sharp whistle that had the two horses trotting over obediently. Maddi didn't have time to be scared of getting back on the horse. She was sitting astride her again before she knew which way was up.

Aristedes made sure to stay close this time, watching La Reina carefully. He was within touching distance of taking the reins again if he had to.

Maddi was occupied just trying to get her scrambled brain back into some kind of order.

Aristedes wanted her.

As much as she wanted him.

But what would happen now? Would he regret this moment of passion with the woman who had upended his world? Would he judge her for being so...wanton? Maybe he was already cursing himself for his own weakness.

What did she want to happen?

Maddi's insides clenched.

She wanted him.

With a desperation that felt almost feverish.

This was the man she'd been waiting for. The passion she'd dreamt of.

The man who is promised in marriage to your half-sister.

Maddi sobered at that.

Surely Laia wouldn't care? After all, she'd spent the last four years doing her best to put this man off marrying her. And she was now completely AWOL in a bid to get to her coronation before they could be married.

Maddi knew Laia wouldn't care. She might care that Maddi had taken leave of her senses, but she wouldn't feel remotely betrayed. If anything, she would see it as Maddi going to extreme lengths to distract the King of Santanger.

Maddi put a hand to her mouth as a little giggle erupted at the thought of Laia encouraging her to seduce the King.

Aristedes looked at her. They were approaching the

arch that led back into the stables. People were milling around in the distance.

'What's funny?'

The full import of what had just happened hit Maddi and she took her hand down and shook her head, suddenly deadly sober again. 'Nothing.'

Grooms came to meet them, but before one of them could help Maddi off the horse Aristedes was there, his hands around her waist. She put her hands on his shoulders and let him take her weight. She slid down and stood. Her legs still weren't entirely steady.

The grooms led the horses away. Maddi could see the security men at a discreet distance. Also one of Aristedes's aides, who looked as if he needed to tell him something. But he was looking at her.

Maddi felt exposed. Conscious of her hair loose and wild.

She wasn't sure how to try and articulate what was in her head. 'Aristedes... I—'

'We have a formal event to attend this evening. Hannah will help you get ready. We leave at six.'

With that, he turned and strode away, his aide hurrying to catch up and walk alongside him. Security men followed.

Hannah appeared in a golf buggy. 'Princess Laia? I'll take you back to your rooms. Would you like a snack before preparing for tonight's event?'

Maddi blinked at the girl. The fact that she'd taken Maddi's healthy appetite into account made Maddi feel absurdly emotional. It was as if a layer of skin had just been removed from her body, leaving her open to the elements.

To emotion.

She realised she was ravenous after the overload of adrenalin and shock and everything that had happened. She smiled at Hannah. 'That would be amazing, thank you.'

The girl smiled. 'I will arrange it, Princess Laia.'

Ari adjusted his bow tie for the umpteenth time. It was perfect. But it felt too tight. He cursed softly and left it alone.

His valet asked, 'Anything else, Your Majesty?'

Ari said, 'No, thank you, Tomas. You can go.'

The man left and Ari looked at his watch. He was ready early. As if he was some eager teenager, going on a date. He scowled at himself and went out to his living area, helping himself to a generous shot of whisky.

The burn down his throat couldn't burn away the memory of the stark, cold panic he'd felt in his guts when he'd seen Maddi clinging on to La Reina for dear life, hurtling towards certain maiming or even death on those rocks.

How he'd managed to get to her on time and bring the horse to a stop was still something he couldn't fathom.

And then he'd pulled her off the horse, fearing the worst... But she'd been okay. She'd been fine. So fine that he hadn't been able to resist the temptation to kiss her.

He took another slug of whisky to try and drown how that had felt, but the alcohol only made the memory burn hotter.

She'd been everything he'd fantasised about. Soft and lush and firm and strong. Hesitant at first, and then matching him stroke for stroke. The weight and feel of her breast in his hand had been more erotic than anything he could remember experiencing in years.

He still couldn't understand where the control to stop had come from. The control not to take her from the beach and give in to the almost overwhelming need to take her there and then on the sand.

The intervening hours had done little to douse his desire. Tasting her had opened the floodgates. He wanted her more than he'd ever wanted another woman. She couldn't be more inappropriate. She couldn't be more off-limits. She was lady-in-waiting to his future wife.

A future wife who is currently hiding in some corner of the world to avoid marrying you, pointed out a small voice.

Right now that fact didn't seem pertinent to Ari. Not as pertinent as how he was going to be able to stand beside Maddi for an entire evening and not give in to the temptation to touch her again.

Kiss her again.

Echoes of memories of his father, doing little to hide his desire for his latest mistress, whispered over Ari like a chill breeze. He'd vowed to be different. He had more control than that. He'd built his life around it.

But on the beach earlier…had shown that perhaps he was as susceptible to a woman as his father had been.

It had been the adrenalin rush, he assured himself now. Maddi could have died.

A shudder went through him again.

There was a knock on the door and then a voice from behind him. 'Your Majesty, Princess Laia is here.'

The back of Ari's neck prickled with awareness. He swore he could smell her scent. His blood heated.

He gritted his jaw. She was just a woman. Like any other. Her aim since she had got here was to drive him insane and he would not allow it. He was in control.

Slowly he turned around and his gaze fell on the woman before him. His hand tightened on the glass in his hand. Faintly he heard a cracking sound.

Dios mio.

Any sense of control Ari had convinced himself he had drained out of his head and body, to be replaced with pure, unadulterated lust and the certain knowledge that no amount of control in the universe would be enough to make him resist this woman.

Maddi hovered self-consciously in the doorway. Aristedes was looking at her with such a fierce expression on his face that she asked, 'Is it not okay? Hannah and the stylist said it was the perfect dress for the event...'

It was a classic black evening gown. Strapless and ruched at the bodice, then falling to the floor in whimsical layers of chiffon. A wide length of chiffon went over one shoulder.

With it she wore a short, simple diamond necklace, matching drop earrings and bracelet. Her hair was smooth and pulled back into a sophisticated chignon, held in place by a diamond pin. When she'd seen herself in the mirror she'd wished she had her phone, so she could send a picture of herself to Laia. Because she'd never looked so...*sleek*.

She'd missed her sister acutely in that moment, because she'd never really had a close girlfriend before and Laia had become her confidante. This was the most time they'd spent apart since Maddi had met her.

From the look on Aristedes's face, he was seriously regretting what had happened earlier. He put down the glass he was holding on the table and said, 'It's fine. We should go.'

He walked towards her, and that was when Maddi took in the full impact of the King in his classic black tuxedo. He was breathtaking. Suave, debonair and dangerous all at once. And yet the image of him in those jeans earlier...the way they'd clung so snugly to his thighs and buttocks...the way he'd sat on the horse... that was even more intoxicating.

He put out a hand, to indicate that she should precede him out of the room, and she walked ahead of him on shaky legs, clutching the little bag that matched the dress.

He didn't attempt to make conversation as they made their way to the chauffeur-driven SUV waiting in the courtyard. Once seated in the back, with Aristedes on the other side of the car, long legs stretched out, Maddi knew she couldn't bear it if there was going to be this much tension between them.

Before she could lose her nerve, she said, 'Look, about earlier...' And there she faltered. Because to put it into words how seismic it had been—what did she even want to say?

Aristedes pressed a button and the privacy screen went up. Maddi flushed. She kept forgetting.

He looked at her. 'What about earlier?'

'I...' She stopped helplessly. Because what she wanted to say was, *I want to do that again.* But clearly

Aristedes had no intention of doing it again. He'd come to his senses.

'Nothing,' she said, making a huge effort to push down her emotions. 'It doesn't matter. What's this event we're attending?'

Aristedes looked relaxed, but Maddi didn't trust it. There was a sudden sense of crackling volatility in the air. As if some silent communication had taken place between them that she was unaware of.

Ignoring her question, he said, 'You were brave, earlier.'

Maddi blinked. She hadn't expected that. 'I was?'

He nodded. 'You got back on the horse again.'

Maddi's face grew hot. 'I was a little…distracted.'

The ghost of a smile made Aristedes's mouth twitch, but Maddi couldn't decipher it before he said, 'Next time I'll give you a proper lesson. I won't leave you alone.'

Maddi's heart thumped. 'Next time?'

'You said you were learning—no reason why you can't keep doing it here.'

'I… Okay.'

Then he smoothly segued into answering her question. 'The event we're attending tonight is an annual charity ball to raise funds for local hospitals.'

Maddi had been to similar events with Laia. Lots of hand-shaking and thanking donors for their generosity.

She said, 'I'll do my best to fade into the background.'

Aristedes made a faint snorting sound. 'Then you shouldn't have worn that dress.'

A sense of exposure gripped Maddi. Was he sending her out to make a complete fool of herself?

'You said it was fine!'

His dark gaze swept her up and down. 'It is fine. It's more than fine. You look…spectacular.'

Maddi's skin prickled all over. Now he didn't look as if he was regretting what had happened at all.

She couldn't help saying, a little plaintively, 'You're very hard to read—do you know that?'

His gaze met hers. 'Shall I make it a little clearer?'

Before she could answer he had reached for her and tugged her gently towards him across the back seat. The dress rustled around her. He snaked an arm around her waist and then cupped her jaw with his other hand, angling her face towards him.

Maddi couldn't breathe. She could see the intensity in his eyes now… Dark gold flecks like little fires burning.

She put her hand over his where he held her, entwined their fingers. On a breath, she reached up and touched her mouth to his, unable to help herself.

For an infinitesimal moment nothing happened. Almost as if Aristedes was testing himself. Testing to see if he could resist her.

But just as she was drawing back, sure he was mocking her, he stopped her movement and stopped her breath with his mouth on hers. It was an open and explicit kiss. He wasn't mocking her. He wanted her.

And she wanted him.

Time and space fell away. There was only this moment and the way it felt to have Aristedes's hard, sensual mouth on hers, tongues duelling, mimicking a far more intimate action. It was a dance that Maddi knew instinctively, even though her experience of kissing up to now had been laughably juvenile.

She'd been kissed. But not like this. Not by a man who kissed *women*. Sensual, experienced women, who could match him. But she wasn't a sensual, experienced woman. She was a virgin playing at being a sensual, experienced woman. Which was easy to do under this man's hands.

Virgin.

Maddi imagined the look of distaste on his face if he ever discovered such a fact. She tensed and pulled back, breathing raggedly. The fact that he looked momentarily disorientated was some comfort. To know she could have an effect on such a man…

He looked over her shoulder and said, 'We're here.'

Maddi's insides swooped as Aristedes put her away from him gently. Thankfully the windows were tinted, because Maddi could already see a throng of press photographers outside a beautiful building with wide steps leading up to an elaborate foyer.

Aristedes got out and there was a roar from the crowd. He was an undeniably popular monarch. Maddi only had seconds to check her make-up before he was opening her door and helping her out.

She'd been to such events with Laia, but had never been the focus of attention until now. She'd have to remember not to look startled.

Aristedes put a hand at her lower back, lightly guiding her up the steps and into the stunning gilded and golden lobby.

CHAPTER SEVEN

ARI COULDN'T CONCENTRATE. That didn't bother him unduly—he could sleepwalk his way through this event. The reason for his lack of concentration was a few feet away, talking to the French ambassador's wife, a little frown between her eyes as she focused on what the woman was saying.

He'd told Maddi on their way in to let him do the talking, lest anyone spend too much time with her and start to get suspicious. Although he was fairly certain most people here wouldn't ever have met the Princess in person. And Maddi certainly looked enough like her to fool all onlookers.

He wondered at that again. They were so alike... could it really just be a coincidence? Simply the fact that they came from the same place? He hadn't heard from his friend Antonio Chatsfield yet—which was unlike him. He made a mental note to chase him up.

He made his excuses to the people around him and went over to Maddi, taking her arm. He felt the way she reacted to his presence, as if a little jolt had gone through her body. A body he had every intention of exploring so thoroughly that she would cease to have this hold over him...

* * *

'She's never been to Santanger or Isla'Rosa before, and she's never met Princess Laia.'

Maddi felt unaccountably defensive after Aristedes had come over to interrupt her conversation with the French ambassador's wife.

'That's not why I pulled you away.'

Maddi looked up at Aristedes. 'It's not?'

He shook his head. 'I pulled you away because we need to be the first on the dance floor.'

Dread pooled in Maddi's belly as Aristedes led her into another room, where the sounds of a waltz enveloped them. Laia had told Maddi about the endless hours of dance practice she'd had to endure when growing up.

She hissed at Aristedes, 'I've never danced like this before. I don't know what to do.'

If people didn't already suspect she might not be Princess Laia, then surely when they saw her wooden dance movements they'd guess in an instant.

Aristedes, unconcerned, swung her into his arms and said, 'It's fine. Just follow my lead and try to relax.'

Try to relax!

Maddi might have laughed if she hadn't been so terrified. Doing something for the first time, surrounded by hundreds of people scrutinising her every move!

Aristedes's arm was high across her back and he held her hand in his, close to his shoulder. He said again, 'Just relax. Don't look at them—look at me.'

That would be even worse than the hundreds of curious eyes. But she did it, and it worked to an extent. The world narrowed down to Aristedes and those amazing, unfathomable eyes.

A question came to her, unbidden, and it came out of her mouth before she could stop it. 'Does anyone call you Ari?'

'My brother does, and my mother used to call me Ari. Sometimes women would call me Ari, but it was an attempt to foster an intimacy that I didn't appreciate.'

Maddi made a *tsk*-ing sound. 'How cheeky of them.'

To her surprise she realised they were revolving easily around the dance floor, her feet following his. Other couples had joined them now, and the pressure eased a little.

Maddi was curious. 'So, these women...there were a few...?'

'Are you asking me how many lovers I've had?'

Maddi flushed. 'No.'

Yes. And did he have a current lover?

'You're very impertinent.'

Maddi winced. 'I'm sorry. I tend to speak and then think.'

Aristedes's mouth twitched again. She was beginning to love that twitch. That sign that she could make him smile, even a tiny bit.

He said, 'I've had my fair share. I'm not a monk. But I'm not going to violate my wedding vows. Once I'm married I will be faithful to my wife.'

She was surprised at the vehemence in his voice. 'Even if you don't...fancy her?'

He'd told her himself he'd never felt anything like that for Laia.

'Dynastic marriages are built on far more solid foundations than chemistry and emotion. They have to be.'

'Was that what your parents' marriage was like?'

For the first time she felt tension in his body. His jaw clenched.

Maddi said hurriedly, 'Ignore me. I'm asking too many questions.'

But he didn't seem to hear her. He said, 'It should have been. But my mother fell in love with my father. It was an arranged marriage. He didn't love her. He had affairs. Lots of them. No secret. He flaunted them in her face, as if to punish her for the folly of loving him. It destroyed her.'

He looked at her then.

'That's why I have vowed to be faithful to my wife. I won't put her through what my father did to my mother, just because he couldn't control himself.'

He didn't say it, but she heard the words. *He was weak.* Maddi was genuinely moved.

'That must have been so hard to witness.'

'My brother Dax bore the brunt of it. He was closer to my mother. I was occupied with the duties of becoming King one day. She depended on him. Too much.'

Maddi stayed silent. It put his brother into a new perspective. She knew what it was like to grow up with a parent who had suffered great heartbreak. But at least her mother had managed to pull herself out of it and get on with her life.

'What happened to her?' she asked.

'She died in a car crash when I was seventeen. Dax was fifteen.'

So he and his brother had lost both parents within a year of each other.

'I'm sorry, that must have been rough.'

He looked at her. 'Any more questions?'

Maddi shook her head. But then she said, 'I can understand why you'd settle for a passionless marriage now, but you can't control someone's emotions. What if your wife falls in love with you?'

Aristedes smiled mirthlessly. 'I think all signs are pointing to that not being a problem.'

Was he admitting defeat? Giving up on his dogged refusal to acknowledge Laia's reluctance to marry him?

But then he said, 'Even if there was passion…which would certainly make the marriage more palatable… passion doesn't last.'

Maddi struggled to think of examples of passionate, long-lasting relationships, but drew a blank. 'You're very cynical.'

'So would you be if you'd grown up in my world. At least I know not to believe in myths and fairy tales. What a waste of a life.'

No doubt he was referring to his mother. And while Maddi agreed to a certain extent, because she'd always taken a very pragmatic view of love and relationships—largely after seeing her own mother choose to move on and settle down with someone who might not set the world alight, but who loved her and was kind—she felt a surprising need to counter Aristedes's arrogant complacency.

'That's easy to say if you've never actually been in love.'

'How do you know I haven't? I might have been made cynical by a broken heart.'

Maddi ignored the pang near *her* heart at the thought of any woman capturing his.

She snorted. 'I would like to be there on the day

when you're felled by love. I think that would be a very satisfying sight.'

Aristedes didn't even dignify that with a comment. He asked, 'What about you? Have you been in love?'

Maddi shook her head. 'No. And while I hate to admit it, I agree with a lot of what you say. But I'm not arrogant enough to assume I'm immune.'

'I prefer to think of it as realism.'

It was only then that Maddi realised the music was fading out and a new song was starting. They'd stopped moving and were just looking at each other. She became uber-conscious of her body, pressed against his. They fitted. Even though she was almost a foot shorter.

He said, 'By the way, you can call me Ari.'

Her insides swooped. 'Aren't you afraid I might be trying to foster intimacy?'

He shook his head. 'No, because you're not like any other woman I've ever met. And we both know the truth of what's going on here.'

Maddi felt breathless. She chose to interpret his statement that she wasn't like any other woman as a good thing. 'And what *is* going on here, exactly?'

The band was playing something a little jazzier now. Aristedes started moving again.

'A very rare and unusual mutual chemistry. Something that I don't think either of us expected.'

Maddi shook her head. She certainly hadn't expected to still be here, impersonating her sister. She'd only started this with a view to helping Laia escape.

She couldn't take her eyes off his mouth.

'If you keep looking at me like that, I'll be tempted to break protocol.'

She dragged her gaze up. 'What protocol?'

'We can't be seen to be physically intimate before we marry.'

She frowned. 'But…we're not getting married.'

'I know that…you know that. They don't know that.'

As if waking from a trance, Maddi became aware of the avid crowd around them again. People were dancing past them, staring at them as if they were animals in a zoo.

She wanted to duck her head into Aristedes's shoulder. She wanted to ask if they could leave yet. But she clamped her mouth shut. Because if they did leave… what then?

As if hearing her thoughts, he said, 'Much as I would like to, we can't leave yet. There's more meeting and greeting to do.'

Maddi was used to this—albeit to the other side of it. She knew that it was like an endurance sport, and she'd been in awe of Laia's stamina and patience. Now it looked as if she was to be tested to see just how well-suited she was to the role of princess.

A couple of hours later, Maddi was reaching her breaking point. Her feet were killing her. Her face was numb. She was dizzy from all the names and the people she'd met.

An aide approached the King and said something into his ear.

Aristedes put his hand on Maddi's elbow. He looked at her. 'Ready?'

'For what?' She might cry if there was another room to go to, where more people waited to meet them.

'To leave?'

Relief made her weak. 'Yes, please.'

'Try to look a little less delighted,' Aristedes commented dryly.

Maddi schooled her features as they were led out of the elaborate hall and their security followed them as they made their way down to the entrance where the car waited.

Maddi had never been so glad to sit down. She considered herself to be fit—she'd run a half-marathon with Laia in the last year—but this required next-level endurance skills.

In the back of the car, she asked, 'Do you ever get used to this?'

'It's a job, Maddi. And a privilege.'

'That's what Laia—I mean, Princess Laia says.'

'You're close to her.' He said it as a statement.

Maddi nodded. 'She's my best friend, even though I've only known her a year.'

'Clearly you'll do anything for her. You're loyal.'

Maddi shifted uncomfortably. Was she, though? When she was lusting after her sister's intended? Even though Laia had no intention of marrying the man?

The car was winding through the streets of Santanger. Maddi saw people strolling along the pavements. Shops were open late. Restaurants had tables spilling out into picturesque little squares. Down by the marina sleek yachts bobbed on the water, some lit up with fairy lights. An almost full moon hung in the sky, sending out a pearlescent glow.

For some reason Maddi felt incredibly melancholic. She wished... She wasn't even sure what she wished.

And then it hit her. She wished she was here for real. That she could be herself with this man. Not hiding behind a much larger persona.

The fact that no one else seemed to have realised she wasn't Princess Laia made her feel a little invisible...

'Maddi?'

She swallowed the unwelcome lump in her throat. What was wrong with her?

Aristedes took her hand. 'Maddi? What is it? Was tonight too much?'

She looked at him when she felt she could hide her emotion. 'No, it was fine. I was just thinking it's so lovely here. You have a beautiful country.'

'I do. I'm very lucky.'

Impulsively she said, 'You see me, don't you?'

She stopped and bit her lip in case she said anything else.

He frowned. 'Of course I see you. You're sitting just inches away.'

'I mean...you see *me*, Maddi Smith, not Princess Laia.'

Strangely, Ari knew exactly what Maddi meant. Because he had that sensation too. That people only saw King Aristedes. A figurehead. Not the man underneath.

He said, 'The minute I knew you weren't Princess Laia, I saw you.'

Maddi was direct. More relaxed. A little dreamy. Barefoot more often than not. Princess Laia—from what he remembered—was much more reserved. A product of her upbringing, no doubt.

Princess Laia wouldn't bombard him with personal

questions, like Maddi did, with the lack of guile of a child. Questions that he'd answered when he usually cut people off.

A sense of exposure made his skin prickle. He'd told her far too much.

His parents' sordid history was an open secret within the palace, but not among the public—and yet he'd blithely spilled it all to Maddi as if she wasn't here as some sort of Trojan Horse.

For the first time since this woman had impersonated her boss, the Crown Princess, since Ari had realised just how reluctant Laia was to marry him, he had a very fledgling sense of things shifting. Becoming less concrete. Less certain. Not least because he was about to throw caution to the wind and behave as uncharacteristically as he ever had. By ignoring the need to control everything.

Right now, none of that bothered him as much as it should. Because he was distracted by Maddi's eyes. Huge and dark green, with tantalising hints of gold and brown. Glowing with some emotion that, inexplicably, he felt too, even though he couldn't name it.

Didn't want to name it.

What he wanted was far more base and carnal.

He lifted Maddi's hand and tugged her closer. Her scent tickled his nostrils. Light and yet deep at the same time. With some mysterious base note.

'I want you, Maddi.' The words fell from his mouth as easily as breathing.

Her eyes widened. A flush of colour stained her cheeks. She really was beautiful.

'But…is it…? Are we allowed?'

He almost smiled at her question. As if there was a higher power to answer to than him. Any other woman would be sliding into his lap at the merest hint that he wanted her.

'In public we have to be relatively chaste, but within the palace, if we're discreet, we can do what we want. After what the staff there witnessed with my father, an affair between me and my future Queen will be like a Disney movie.'

'An affair...?'

'We're two consenting adults, Maddi. I'm not married yet.'

'But you still intend to get married to Princess Laia...'

Did he? Those doubts he had took root. But Ari wasn't about to reveal his inner vacillations to a woman bent on creating chaos wherever she went. Not least in his body.

He said, 'We have an agreement. If she comes to her senses then, yes, of course I'll marry her. However, if she won't agree to the marriage then I'll have to choose another bride of royal blood. I will be getting married, no matter what. I have to.'

'You have to marry a bride of royal blood?'

Ari nodded. He really didn't want to talk about this. That was all in the future. He was more interested in the present. Vastly more interested.

But his conscience compelled him to say, 'You know nothing can come of this, Maddi. I will marry according to my duty and my responsibility and I will not betray my vows. This can only be temporary.'

The car was pulling to a stop in the main palace

courtyard. Ari could see the staff waiting to jump into action.

Maddi pulled her hand back. He felt her distance herself. Physically and emotionally.

Ari signalled discreetly to the staff not to disturb them. Well-worn cynicism told him she was sensing an opportunity to bargain for something in return for agreeing to this affair. Now that he'd laid out in no uncertain terms that she would never become a favoured mistress.

He'd been through this with lovers before. Usually when he ended things.

She said, 'I don't know if it's a good idea… There's a lot of…stuff between us.'

Ari felt a sense of disappointment snake through him. He really had thought she was different. More fool him. The woman had been playing him since she'd arrived.

He leaned back. 'What is it you want, Maddi?'

She looked at him. Blinked. Long lashes cast shadows on her cheeks. 'What are you talking about?'

'This game you're playing now that you know the parameters of our relationship.'

She shook her head. Her face looked pale.

Ari ignored it.

She said, 'What *game*? I wouldn't know how to play a game even if I was given a rule book.'

'Says the woman who worked in a casino?'

Maddi's eyes widened. Her mouth opened. 'You know what? I've changed my mind. You're the last man I would ever have an affair with. You're a cynical, arrogant—'

Maddi's door was opened unceremoniously and she almost fell out. An unwitting staff member obviously hadn't seen the signal not to disturb them.

Ari cursed, the feeling of having made a mistake already curdling in his gut as he saw Maddi scramble inelegantly out of the car to get away from him.

Because he realised what he'd seen in her expression along with shock just now. *Hurt.*

By the time he had stepped out and caught up with her it was obvious she was steaming mad. Ari took her elbow. She was stiff as a board.

He said tersely, 'Just keep walking and don't cause a scene.'

Miraculously, she did as he asked. They reached his private rooms and he dismissed his valet for the night.

Once they were alone, Maddi pulled away from his hand and stalked into the reception room. She whirled around. 'How *dare* you insinuate that I'm on the make for something?' She hitched up her chin. 'I grew up with just enough to get by once my education was paid for, and I've worked for every cent I ever earned. I still do. I don't expect a handout from anyone.'

Ari's gut clenched. Either she was an undiscovered award-winning actress or he'd read this very wrong. He ran a hand through his hair. He didn't usually find himself apologising to anyone.

'Look, I think I've misread the situation...'

'You *think*?'

Maddi had her hands on her hips now. She reminded him of how she'd been that first evening she'd been here, when she'd thrown the phone out of the window. Magnificent and strong. Defiant.

He put his hands out. 'Okay, I'm sorry. I definitely misread the situation. I just… I'm used to people wanting things from me.'

Maddi looked slightly less angry. She folded her arms across her chest, which only had the effect of pushing her breasts upwards. Ari valiantly kept his gaze up.

'I guess I can understand that. You're a wealthy man. A king. I know not everyone is…'

'As pure as you?' Ari supplied.

She looked at him and all the colour in her cheeks leached away, leaving her looking stricken.

He walked forward. 'What is it? What did I say?'

She shook her head. 'Nothing. I'm…fine. Look, I don't want anything from you, Ari. All I want is for Princess Laia to get what she wants—which is not to become your wife.'

Ari ignored the bit about Princess Laia. He moved closer. 'You're lying, Maddi.'

She glared at him. She looked as if she wanted to stamp her foot.

'What will it take to prove to you that I want nothing?'

Ari reached out and plucked the pin from her hair, making it tumble down around her shoulders, thick and wild. Understanding dawned in her eyes.

'Okay, fine…there is something I want,' she admitted grudgingly.

Every nerve in Ari's body tingled at being so close to her but not touching her yet. 'What's that?'

She looked up at him and his control wavered dangerously. Did she have any idea how she was looking at him? With a provocative expression of hunger mixed with awe mixed with something else he couldn't figure out.

She bit her lip for a second, and then she said in a rush, 'I want to be touched by you. Kissed. Made love to.'

'I want you, Maddi…more than I've ever wanted anyone else.'

She shook her head. 'You don't have to say that. I know what this is…you've made that very clear.'

But even if Ari had tried, he couldn't have stopped the words spilling out. This woman made him utter things he'd never have dreamt of saying to anyone else before.

He reached out and trailed his fingers along her jaw. A delicate line. But strong. She quivered under his touch. He burned.

CHAPTER EIGHT

A MOMENT AGO Maddi had been so angry with this man and now… Now she was ready to dissolve in a pool of lust at his feet. If he hadn't looked genuinely contrite for accusing her of being some sort of gold-digger she might not still be here. But she'd had the very real sense that whatever she'd said had triggered him into a response he'd given many times before.

With his other lovers.

Maddi pushed that toxic thought down. She was no different from them—she knew that. But right now she didn't care, because she wanted him. Desperately. She wanted him to be her first lover.

When he'd joked that not everyone was as pure as her just now she'd nearly given herself away. Spectacularly. Would he know she was a virgin? Surely by now it wouldn't be that obvious?

His hand dropped from her jaw and, without taking his eyes off her face, he undid his bow tie and drew it off, throwing it aside. He undid the top button of his shirt. She saw dark skin, a hint of hair.

She almost whimpered. But a sliver of doubt sneaked in like a cold breeze, dousing her feverish desire. More than a sliver. She wasn't ready for a man like Aristedes. He had the wrong idea about her. He obviously thought she was experienced. A woman of the world. The kind of woman who would nonchalantly go to his room with him and be able to do things that would please him...

Because she would want to please him.

But how could she possibly please him?

The fear of disappointing him was acute.

She forced herself to meet his eye. Regret was already burning her insides like bile. 'I'm so sorry, Aristedes... I'm truly not playing any games... I just think this isn't a good idea.'

His face was suddenly expressionless. His eyes shuttered. He said nothing for a long moment and then he took a step back. 'As you wish. If you change your mind, you know where I am.'

He turned and walked towards his bedroom suite and Maddi fled back to her rooms before she changed her mind. She went inside and leaned against the door.

What she'd just walked away from was seismic.

Ari saw her.

She knew he did. Even if his cynicism had got in the way briefly. And he wanted *her*, which was intoxicating.

For her whole life Maddi had felt somewhat invisible. She'd been acutely conscious of her mother's sadness, and conscious that it had to do with her. So she'd tried to make herself smaller, so as not to cause any more sadness.

She'd learnt not to ask too many questions about her father, but had pored over his image online and that of her half-sister, fascinated by their resemblance while knowing that they were a world apart.

It had always hurt to know that her sister had had a relationship with their father. There was a picture that Maddi had come across online, of her sister and father on a boat, fishing. Laia was about ten years old, laughing up into the King's face. He was smiling down at her indulgently. Maddi had printed it out and kept it for years—a bittersweet reminder that he hadn't wanted to know her.

When she'd told Laia about it, Laia had cried.

Maddi kicked off her shoes and padded barefoot over to the dressing room, removing her jewellery and putting it back carefully in the boxes. The diamonds twinkled at her benignly.

She felt keyed up. Restless. About as far from being able to sleep as it was possible to feel. She looked at herself in the mirror. Flushed cheeks. Wide eyes. Yearning. Aching. Pulse throbbing. Still.

She couldn't believe she'd stood up to the King like that. Called him out on his cynicism. And he'd admitted he was wrong. It had been exhilarating.

She wanted him.

Would it really be so selfish to savour this moment of someone really seeing her. Appreciating her? To take this one thing for herself, ready or not? To give her innocence to the man who had already fulfilled her fantasy of what a passionate awakening might feel like?

Sooner or later she would have to leave here. She would never see Aristedes again. Because she knew his marriage with Laia would never happen. Laia would persuade him to agree to a more modern peace agreement—Maddi knew she would. And he would weather this change in his plans and get on with his life, choose a new bride of royal blood...sire his heirs. He might *want* his Queen. He might even fall in love with his Queen, in spite of his cynical arrogance.

You have royal blood, whispered a voice.

Maddi went still. She was a princess. Albeit very much in secret. But suddenly she couldn't stop thinking of the tantalising possibility of telling Ari that she was also a princess of Isla'Rosa. That perhaps he might agree to switch marrying Laia for Maddi.

She caught her expression in the mirror, smiling moonily at herself, and immediately stopped and scowled. What on earth was wrong with her? She'd met the man scarcely a week ago and, yes, she had a crush on him, but was she really fantasising about offering herself up to him as a substitute royal wife? Before the people of Isla'Rosa even knew she was a princess? Offering herself up to a man who was cynical and jaded? Who had admitted that he was more than happy to have a marriage in name only. To breed the next generation with no hint of scandal or drama.

She wasn't ready to be a queen! She could barely get her head around being a princess. And who was to say he would choose her even if he knew she was of royal blood?

Her blood curdled at the thought. *Rejection.* All over again. She wouldn't risk that for anyone.

Maddi might have sown doubts in his head about his marriage to Laia, but there was no way she could risk revealing her full identity in case he used it against her. To lure Laia out of hiding. Or, worse, to create a scandal in Isla'Rosa by revealing her identity to the people before Laia had had a chance to do so.

It was Laia's narrative to control, revealing Maddi's true heritage as her half-sister, and Maddi would not betray her wishes. After all, she was loyal to Isla'Rosa too.

But in the meantime Maddi couldn't deny that she did want something from King Aristedes. Now more than ever. Because she fully realised how finite this was. And how much he would potentially hate her when he found out who she really was. That she'd been hiding her identity as a princess.

He wouldn't understand that she was still getting used to the concept. It wasn't as if she took it for granted. She knew that until Laia actually acknowledged her birth in front of the people of Isla'Rosa she wouldn't feel as if she truly was of royal blood.

And that betraying little fantasy she'd had of him choosing her to be his Queen instead of Laia? It would be buried deep down, where she'd buried all her very secret fantasies that perhaps things might be different for her, that she might experience a great love some day, even though she'd ruined her mother's chances for love.

So for now she was still a regular person, and suddenly things were very clear. Maddi knew she would always regret not taking the chance to be with Aristedes. To know his touch. To surrender her innocence to him. To let him be the one to initiate her in the ways of being a woman.

Maddi stopped thinking. She turned from the mirror and walked back to the door, opened it and walked out. Guided by sheer desire, Maddi retraced her steps back down the corridor and to Aristedes's rooms.

The guards were outside. Wordlessly, one of them

opened the door. Vaguely Maddi computed this, and what it must mean.

He'd told them to let her in if she came back.

Maddi went into the suite. There were a few lamps throwing out golden light. It was silent. She saw a light coming from the bedroom area and walked over, barefoot.

She stood in the doorway and saw Aristedes's clothes draped haphazardly over a chair. It was only then that she registered the steam coming from under another door. The bathroom. And then he emerged, looking down as he tied a knot in the towel slung low on his hips.

He was bare-chested, and Maddi's gaze was glued to that area. The well-defined pectorals. A light smattering of dark hair. The six-pack that looked as if it had been painted in shade and light by Michelangelo. Not an ounce of spare flesh. His skin was still damp. Gleaming.

Then he spoke. 'Are you really here?'

Maddi looked up. He'd seen her. He was frowning. Hair slicked back. The bones of his face stark and beautiful.

She nodded. 'I... I think so.'

'Come here.'

Maddi walked over, the dress pooling around her bare feet, softly swishing against her legs. She stopped about a foot away from Aristedes. He reached out and traced a finger down her cheek. Took a length of hair and let it run through his fingers.

'You're real...' he breathed.

It soothed something inside her that he wasn't behaving as if he'd just been waiting for her inevitable return. He looked as stunned as she felt to be doing this.

Unable to resist the temptation, she reached out and placed her palm flat against Aristedes's chest. It was warm and hard. His heart thumped under her hand. Strong. Her little finger grazed a nipple and he sucked in a breath, putting his hand over hers, trapping it.

He reached for her with his other arm, pulling her closer. He looked down. 'Barefoot?'

She nodded. He smiled. She melted inside. Then he cupped her face in his hands and tilted it up, his gaze roving over her features hungrily for a few seconds before his mouth touched hers. A light kiss at first. A testing…a tasting. But Maddi was hungry. She moved closer and wrapped her arms around his neck, bringing their bodies flush together.

She could feel the heat from his body seeping through the thin material of the dress. Her breasts felt heavy.

The kiss changed and became harder. One of Aristedes's hands caught the back of her head and an arm wrapped around her back, holding her. Which was good, because she wasn't sure her legs were still working.

The kiss became deeper and more explicit, stoking the fire in Maddi's blood. Tongues tangled. She bit his lower lip gently, experimentally. It was firm. She soothed it with her tongue and Aristedes growled low in his throat.

He pulled back. Maddi opened her eyes. Everything was blurry. He slowly came back into focus and the look on his face made her gulp. He looked…ravenous. She felt a moment of insecurity—should she tell him she wasn't exactly experienced? But then she imagined him looking shocked, and then maybe disgusted... Selfishly, she didn't want to risk it.

Surely he wouldn't notice?

He moved back slightly and said, 'Turn around.'

Maddi did, and felt him move her hair so that it fell over one shoulder, baring her back. Instead of going straight for the zip, she felt him trace her shoulder blades and then down the centre of her spine to the top of her dress.

She bit her lip to stop a shiver of pure desire. She was dealing with a maestro here, which was immediately intimidating but also reminded her that he'd had lots of practice. And that reminded her that in comparison she was hardly likely to make an impression, no matter how much he might want her.

Her mind spiralled right up until his fingers found the zip and started to pull it down. Then she stopped breathing.

His hands brought the zip all the way down to just above her buttocks. The dress fell away from her breasts. He tugged it gently over her hips and it dropped in a soft swish of silk and chiffon layers at her feet.

Now she wore only a strapless bra and matching lace panties. Aristedes walked around her and stopped in front of her. She couldn't look at him. He tipped up her chin with a finger.

'Breathe, Maddi.'

She sucked in a breath and it went straight to her head. Meanwhile, Aristedes's gaze was moving down, over her chest to her belly and waist, her hips, thighs, legs… She felt his touch like the lick of a flame, leaving sparks wherever it landed.

He looked back up. 'You are more than I could have imagined…'

Maddi swallowed. 'So are you.'

She wanted to touch him again, but she was shy. She curled her hands into fists at her sides.

He took one of her hands and uncurled it. Then he stepped close and reached around her to unsnap her bra in a movement so slick and deft that she only realised what he'd done when a tiny breeze skated over her bare flesh.

Her bra lay on the ground.

Aristedes's gaze got even hotter.

Maddi could feel her nipples puckering into tight buds. He came close again and cupped her breasts in his hands, taking their weight. She had to put her hands on his arms to stay standing. A tremble was starting up somewhere near her knees and travelling up her body, uncontrollable.

Aristedes's thumbs found her nipples and grazed them, back and forth. Maddi gripped his arms tight.

'Aristedes…'

She wasn't even sure what she was asking for. An end to the torture? For it never to stop?

'I told you…call me Ari.'

She looked at him. Her eyes were heavy-lidded. She felt like a cat, wanting to push herself into his hands, begging for heavier petting.

'Ari…'

He lifted his gaze from her breasts. 'Hmm…?'

'I…' She literally couldn't articulate what she needed.

He seemed to take pity on her. He led her over to the massive bed and instructed her, 'Lie back.'

Maddi did. Glad not to have to try and stay standing when she was about to collapse into a puddle at his feet. She looked at the towel around his waist and the prominent bulge. Heat throbbed between her legs. Slick.

He came down over her on his arms. Muscles tensing and bunching. She couldn't help it. She had to touch him. She ran a hand over his chest again, her fingers tracing muscles, her nail snagging on a nipple.

Ari's head lowered and his breath feathered against the skin near her jaw. He pressed a kiss there, and then trailed kisses down her neck to her shoulder. Down further. She tensed when he came to rest beside her. He cupped one breast again, and flicked out his tongue against the sensitive peak. Maddi's back arched at the exquisite sensation. Then he surrounded it with his mouth and the sucking, dragging heat almost sent her into orbit. His other hand moved over her ribcage and down, over her belly, to the top of her lacy briefs.

Maddi couldn't think. She wanted so many things. All at once.

There was a faint ripping noise and Ari had dispensed with her underwear. Now she was completely naked. At his mercy. Begging him with incoherent words… His hand moved between her thighs, pushing them apart gently and then exploring through the heat right into the centre of her body, where she ached the most.

Ari said something that Maddi couldn't understand, but it sounded guttural. Then he took his hand away saying, 'I have to taste you…'

She let out a little whimper and lifted her head to see Ari taking her thighs and spreading them wide. Looking at her with such hunger that it sent a fresh wave of lust through her.

Then he moved down and pressed kisses along each thigh, higher and higher, until he reached the apex of her legs, where she was weeping with heat. He put his mouth to her, exploring that heat. His tongue laved her secret folds and Maddi was done...

She was so far beyond any realm of what she had thought might happen that when Ari flicked his tongue against her she came in a wild rush of climaxes that seemed to go on for ever, rolling like waves through her whole body.

When the storm had ebbed away, she could feel little after-tremors still rippling deep inside her. She lifted her head and saw Ari standing looking at her. Eyes burning like obsidian.

He flicked the towel off his waist and Maddi looked down. A sound came out of her mouth that she had no control over. He was...magnificent. A virile male in his prime. She could feel her body weeping for him all over again.

He opened a drawer in a console by the bed and she watched as he sheathed himself with protection.

Good, she thought dimly, *because any hope I had of being responsible or sane has long since left the building.*

He came down over her on his hands again. Moved between her legs. Maddi's heart rate was triple its normal speed, and even though she'd just climaxed, she could feel tension coiling tight again.

Ari put his hand on her, just above her chest, and

trailed it down over one breast, then the other, reigniting the fire with little more than a touch. His hand moved down over her belly, which quivered at his touch, and between her legs.

His eyes flared. 'You're so responsive, *amada*.'

Maddi wanted to beg. But just as she was about to open her mouth Ari took his hand away and moved himself between her legs. She could feel him *there*, about to breach her body, and she moved slightly, hips circling.

In the next second he had thrust into her, in one devastating movement, stealing her breath and her soul. She gasped and put her hands on his hips, momentarily resisting his body. He was big. She felt so stretched. It bordered on being painful.

Ari stopped and said, 'Maddi...?'

She knew instinctively that the pain would only be alleviated if she moved—and she did. Ari sank in deeper. He moved slowly at first, out and then in, letting their bodies get used to one another, sliding and slick. He gathered pace and Maddi no longer felt any discomfort. Only a need for *more*.

And then he was there, hitting the spot that finally gave her some relief, and the building tension was spiralling out of control, too fast for Maddi to hold on. She couldn't stop the fall, nor the onslaught of another wave of pleasure so intense that she cried out, over and over again, hands clasping Ari's shoulders, legs wrapping around his hips as if that might contain it somehow.

Ari's own movements became more frenzied, and eventually he stilled as the storm went through him too. She could feel it in her body and could only absorb it, too spent to do anything else.

* * *

Ari extricated himself from Maddi's embrace—exquisite torture—and lay back on the bed beside her. Her eyes were closed, lashes long on her cheeks. Dark hair was spread around her head. Her body was still flushed. It was the most erotic sight he'd ever seen.

What had just happened had been the most profound experience. He tried to deny it—but he struggled to remember a time when a woman had turned him on so much that the entire world might have fallen away and he wouldn't have noticed or cared.

In a bid to try and make his brain start functioning again, he got out of the bed and went over to his French doors, opening them silently and stepping out onto the terrace. It was completely private here. The night air—cool and fresh—made his skin prickle. He sucked in the salty tang of the sea air.

He heard a noise behind him and turned around to see Maddi stir. She came up on one elbow, looking sexily dishevelled and very well loved.

He moved back to the doorway and she saw him. He watched how her gaze travelled down and widened on the part of his anatomy already responding again. As if he hadn't just died a small death.

But he wasn't going to indulge again now, much as he might like to. The woman who had turned his world upside down from the moment he'd laid eyes on her and assumed she was someone else, was still hiding secrets.

Maddi felt ridiculously shy, considering what had just happened. She couldn't quite wrap her head around it. It was too huge, too seismic.

Ari was standing by the door that led outside to the terrace. The cool night breeze traced over Maddi's skin, making it pucker. He was naked. And it was hard not to be distracted by that amazingly powerful body. She couldn't imagine standing naked in front of him like that, but he was completely unashamed.

Then he came towards the bed and held out a hand. 'Come on.'

Maddi let him pull her up from the bed, a little bemused. Her head was still feeling fuzzy after an overload of pleasure.

He led her into the bathroom and leant into the shower, turning it on. Steam soon filled the space. Ari stepped in and pulled her with him. The powerful spray covered them both and Ari put her in front of him. He poured some soap into his hands before running them all over her body. She was glad she was facing away from him, because she hadn't expected this.

She didn't know what she'd expected, because she hadn't thought that far ahead, but it wasn't this…this tender, post-coital ablution.

He massaged shampoo into her hair and worked his hands over her scalp, long fingers moving slowly and rhythmically. She wanted to lean back against him and slide to the floor at his feet. But then he rinsed the soap from her body and her hair and turned off the shower. The heat and steam dissipated. Ari wrapped a large towel around Maddi's shoulders. Then he got another towel and handed it to her for her hair.

They hadn't spoken a word.

He rubbed himself dry briskly and Maddi wrapped

up her long hair in a towel, turban-like, and secured the other towel under her arms, tying it in a knot.

Ari went into the bedroom, and when Maddi followed him he was pulling on a pair of loose sweats. They hung low on his hips.

He looked at her across the room, and then he said, 'Why didn't you tell me you were a virgin?'

CHAPTER NINE

ARI FOLDED HIS arms across his chest. Partly because he was afraid that he'd reach out and twitch that towel from around Maddi's body and take her back to bed. Her legs were long and shapely, and he had a sudden vivid flashback to how she'd wrapped them around his waist and he'd sunk so deep into her—

He gritted his jaw tight.

His question hung in the air between them. He could see the colour leach from her face. How her eyes widened.

Very faintly, she said, 'I thought you wouldn't notice.'

When Ari thought of how he'd felt every single ripple of her body against his, and how explosive it had been, it made him irrationally irritable.

'How old are you?'

'Twenty-three.'

'How the hell are you still a virgin?'

She hitched up her chin. 'That's not really any of your business.'

Ari wanted to laugh. '*Cariño*, we've just been as intimately acquainted as two people can get. I think I deserve an answer.' Then he ran a hand through his hair. 'I could have hurt you, Maddi. *Dios.*'

Her chin came down. 'You didn't hurt me…it was the opposite.'

Unable to stop himself, Ari closed the distance between them. 'What was it, then?'

She looked up at him. Eyes flecked with dark gold. 'It was…amazing. I didn't… I mean, I haven't before now because I've never met anyone I wanted to be with… like that. I went to an all-girls school,' she went on. 'So I never really had a boyfriend. And then I was working, and the men there were either creepy or just…immature. I didn't go to college, so I never got to have any experience of mixing with guys…otherwise it probably would have happened. As time went on, I just felt like I wanted to hold out for the right person…'

The thought of Maddi sleeping with another man—of another man experiencing her incredible responsiveness and sensual surrender—made Ari feel almost violent.

He said, 'And was I the right person?'

Arrogantly, Ari knew the answer to that—he felt it in his blood. A deep satisfaction he'd never experienced before.

Maddi nodded. 'The moment I saw you… I felt it. The attraction.'

He had too. Which was when he should have realised something was up—because he'd never been attracted to Princess Laia.

So why are you so intent on marrying her?

The doubts whispered to Ari, growing stronger. He

pushed them down. Not the time. Not when he had more interesting things to do.

'Why didn't you tell me?'

'I was afraid you wouldn't want to sleep with me.'

Ari shook his head and admitted, 'I don't think wild horses could have held me back…but I would have had reservations.'

'Why?'

'Because first experiences can be intense, and it's easy to believe that emotions are involved when it's just a physical act.'

'Is that what happened to you?'

Ari wondered how they'd got here, but he said, 'Briefly. My first lover was an older woman. She was beautiful and experienced and quite mesmerising. I thought I was in love, but she soon disabused me of that idea. And when I found out my father had asked her to initiate me, I'd never felt so humiliated in my life.'

Maddi's eyes were huge and full of emotion. 'How could he do such a thing? That's a horrific crossing of boundaries and a betrayal of trust. And as for her? There are names for people like her.'

Ari could see that she was genuinely angry, and it made him feel for a moment as if he'd lost his footing. As if he was on shaky ground.

'It was a long time ago. In the past.'

'You loved this woman?'

Ari shook his head, an old feeling of anger surfacing briefly. 'No. I was momentarily infatuated.'

Maddi bit her lip, and Ari had to restrain himself from reaching out to release that plump flesh. She said, 'So you're telling me this—?'

'Because you asked.'

She made a face. And then, 'You're telling me not to fall in love with you?'

'If you can help it.'

Now she rolled her eyes, but he saw she was suppressing a smile. To Ari's surprise, he felt a lightness bubble up inside him. A lightness he didn't feel very often. The only person who made him feel light was his brother Dax. It was an uncomfortable revelation.

He pushed it aside for now. Along with all the other things he didn't want to think about. Like how he'd already spelled out what this relationship was, but now he was teasing her about it.

She said, 'I'll do my best not to fall for you, Your Majesty.'

'Good,' he said, as he moved closer, not able to resist temptation any more.

He reached for Maddi's towel and loosened it, so that it fell to her feet. Then he took the towel from her head and her hair fell in damp dark skeins around her shoulders, long enough to touch her breasts.

'Because we both know that this situation is just a very unique temporary hiatus in our lives.'

She was breathing fast now, her breasts rising and falling, making Ari's hands itch. But before he could touch her she'd put her hands on his sweatpants and tugged them over his hips and down. He stepped out of them. They were both naked.

He led her back to the bed and told himself that this ravenous hunger was purely due to the novelty of having a new lover. Quite possibly his last lover before marriage. It wasn't specifically unique to Maddi Smith.

Because thinking about the consequences of her being different from any other lover was not something he was prepared to contemplate.

A few days later, Maddi was looking at the tabloid pictures of her and Ari that had been taken at the charity event the other evening. The evening they'd made love. His hand was on the small of her back and her face was turned to look up at him. She was smiling, and his mouth was on the verge of a smile as he looked at her. The headline said: *The look of love between King Aristedes and his future Queen!*

Amazing how misleading pictures could be…

But she knew the reality behind them. The reality being that she wasn't Princess Laia and she shouldn't be here. She was only here to try and stop Ari tracking down Laia with one hundred percent of his focus, but that was fast becoming far too easy to forget.

Especially after the other night.

Maddi put down the papers and went to the terrace and breathed in the fresh, fragrant air deeply. She hadn't slept in her own bed since the other night. Hannah had subtly moved her things to Ari's suite, and since then it had been a blur of making love, having food delivered to Ari's rooms and periodic breaks before indulging in their ravenous hunger for each other over and over again.

He only went to his office when she was sleeping.

Was it always this…intense? It almost scared Maddi how much she wanted Ari. He'd awoken something in her that she'd never even thought she possessed. A carnal hunger. She revelled in this new incarnation of herself, revelled in his touch. She craved him. And even though she knew this phase would fade, it didn't feel as if it was fading any time soon. Only getting stronger.

She had come back here to her own suite under the pretext of needing to find something, but the truth was that she needed some space and time to get her head around what was happening.

She was having an affair with her sister's fiancé. Except she knew that she wasn't really betraying Laia. If anything, she was giving her sister an even more solid reason to turn around and declare their agreement null and void.

She wondered if the newspaper pictures would reach Laia, wherever she was. Would she feel confident enough to return to Isla'Rosa? Had Dax found her? Was that why there was no contact? Maddi knew Laia was resourceful—she'd been successfully avoiding Ari for four years—so if Dax had found her, Maddi wouldn't be surprised if she'd managed to take him by surprise...

There was a sound from the room behind her and Maddi turned around. Ari was walking towards her, in a dark suit with a light shirt, open at the neck. She drank him in helplessly, her body already reacting, softening, moistening, aching for him.

'Here you are.'

He stopped and looked at her. There hadn't been anything planned today, so she'd thrown on a pair of loose trousers and a cropped silk top.

He said, 'Do you want a riding lesson?'

A momentary frisson of fear as she recalled the terror of being on that out-of-control horse made her tense, but she refused to let it stop her. 'I'd like that.'

'Good. The horses will be ready in an hour—they're being groomed at the moment. Which leaves us just enough time...'

'Time for what?'

He came and slid his hands around her waist, finding her bare skin. Maddi's heart picked up pace.

He bent his head and said, close to her mouth, before he kissed her, 'Time for *this*.'

Maddi was fast being pulled under, weakly pushing aside all the things she'd been thinking about. This shouldn't be her reality. But with Ari's mouth on hers and his hands finding her tender flesh and making her moan, she really wanted to believe that it was.

'We're going to a what?' Maddi asked, feeling a sense of panic at what Ari had just said.

She knew he'd told her earlier, but she'd been distracted because he'd been kissing her at the time.

'A walkabout. People line the streets and we literally walk about and meet them. It's in a port town on the other side of the island. It'll be a chance for the more remote islanders to meet you.'

'Are you sure that's a good idea? I mean...it's not like they'll be meeting *me* again. Or Princess Laia.'

But Ari said, 'Until I hear from Princess Laia that she is breaking the agreement, everything is on track for her becoming Queen of Santanger.'

Maddi mentally shook her head at his refusal to believe his plans could be derailed. She had to admire his self-belief. But then, could he even be a king without an inflated sense of self-belief?

Hannah had dressed Maddi in a colourful, flowy silk dress, with buttons down the front and a wide belt. It was chic and elegant. Her hair had been pulled back into a low ponytail and she was relieved to see she'd be wearing comfortable wedges and not impractical high heels. She didn't know how Laia did these things for hours in four-inch heels.

In the car, on their way to the town, they drove over the central mountains and Maddi got a sense of how much bigger Santanger was than Isla'Rosa.

The other side of the mountain led to more fertile lands. Maddi saw fields filled with trees laden down with lemons and oranges. And olive trees. There were vineyards as far as the eye could see. It was abundantly clear that Santanger was a thriving kingdom on all levels.

They passed through picturesque villages with central squares. People going about their business. It felt quaint and old-fashioned but modern all at once. And then the sea came into view again and they drove along winding cliff roads with precipitous drops on one side.

Ari noticed her expression and said, 'I take it you're not a fan of heights?'

'I don't mind them usually, but this is a little…close to the edge.' She looked at him suspiciously. 'You're doing this on purpose, to freak me out.'

He barked out a laugh. 'Not at all. Actually, I'd usually travel by helicopter, but sometimes I like the drive…to keep an eye on things. And I thought you might like to see more of the island.'

Maddi was inordinately touched by his easy thoughtfulness. He was proud of his country. That much was glaringly obvious. And she had to agree it was beautiful.

She quashed the little voice telling her she was being disloyal to Laia.

When they entered the surprisingly large and thriving port town Maddi was surprised—she had imagined a sleepy little fishing village. There was even a stunning Baroque cathedral, very like the one in Santanger, which dominated the main square in the city.

'For a short time in the Middle Ages, when we were being attacked on the southern shore, this town became the capital. It's known for its ancient Roman ruins. The Romans obviously had a similar idea at one point.'

Maddi heard the crowds before she saw them. Another little lurch of panic went into her gut.

She said, 'What do I do?'

'Shake hands and take their gifts. They just want to see you.'

They car came to a stop and Ari got out. The crowds cheered.

Maddi had never seen so many people in one place behind barriers.

He helped her out and she forced down the panic. He led her over to where the people were waiting and the roar was almost deafening. And then it started—a refrain that made Maddi's ears ring.

'Princess Laia, over here! Please! Princess Laia!'

So Maddi did all she could, and dived in. At first it felt forced, pasting a smile on her face to greet these people who were complete strangers, but then she relaxed. They were all so happy and had such kind faces.

Babies were lifted up to her, and as she took one young girl about one year old into her arms, she was surprised at the sudden yearning that pierced her. She'd never considered herself maternal, even though she liked children a lot. But this baby was cherubic. And then she smiled and patted Maddi's cheek with a sticky hand. Everyone laughed and Maddi handed the baby back with genuine regret. She realised she would never be here again, to see her become a little girl and grow older.

Faces blurred into other faces and Maddi's hand felt numb. She'd had so many selfies taken, and accepted and passed back so many flowers and gifts that she was dizzy. But by the time Ari came over to join her from his side of the street and put an arm around her waist, she was euphoric.

A person called out, 'When is the wedding?'

Maddi tensed. But Ari answered easily.

'As you can see, I'm enjoying getting to know my fiancée. An announcement will be made soon.'

The crowd cheered. But it tempered Maddi's happiness as they walked back to the car.

When they were in the car and pulling away, Ari saw her expression and said, 'What's wrong? That went well. They loved you.'

'Yes, but I'm not who they think I am. They liked me because I'm a regular person.'

You're a princess.

Maddi pushed the reminder down. Ari would not appreciate that titbit of information. Not now and not ever, she suspected.

It caused a maelstrom of emotions inside her. Pride

to know that perhaps she *could* do this princess thing—she'd really enjoyed today. But also a sense of yearning to be Princess Maddi, at Ari's side legitimately.

Which would never happen. Because she wouldn't ever have the bravery to risk that rejection. It would destroy her. She knew that it would destroy her. Because she was very much afraid that this crush was developing into something far deeper and more permanent.

No, she told herself desperately, going cold. It couldn't be. She didn't believe in it. It was chemistry... sex. *Not love.*

'Maddi? You look as if you've just seen a ghost.'

She shook her head, struggled to regain her composure. 'It's...just been a long day.'

He took her hand. 'You were a natural. Not many people could deal with a situation like that and connect with the people, but you did.'

Maddi swallowed the lump in her throat. He had no idea how profoundly moving that was to hear.

'Thank you,' she finally managed to get out, without sounding too wobbly.

She saw that they weren't following the cliff road again and Ari said, 'We'll be back at the palace soon. We're taking the helicopter. We wouldn't see much from the car as the light is failing.'

Maddi was relieved. This whole day had been an emotional rollercoaster. 'That sounds practical.'

The helicopter trip over the island was another vision. Little pockets of villages lit up here and there. Wider roads through the middle of the island and around the edge.

The city of Santanger glittered like a bauble. Again,

Maddi saw that it was bigger than she'd thought, meandering high into the hills. In the city there were wide main streets and then smaller warrens of medieval streets. The cathedral was spot-lit.

They landed on the helicopter pad at the back of the palace and Maddi—once all the adrenalin had gone—realised she was exhausted.

Ari led her back to his rooms. He said apologetically, 'I need to take a call for a few minutes—do you mind?'

Maddi shook her head and stifled a yawn. She was also starving hungry, but fatigue won out. She took off the light jacket over her dress and pulled her hair tie out. She lay down on the bed, telling herself it would just be for a moment...

When Ari came back to his bedroom a short time later, he stopped in his tracks. Maddi was lying on the bed, on her side, curled up almost foetally. Hair fanned out around her head. Face resting on her hands. Breathing deeply.

It was the first time he'd been with a woman long enough to have this kind of a relationship. Most of his affairs had been brief, and had not ever encouraged any kind of domesticity. No lover would have dared to fall asleep in his company unless sex had been involved! And even then he hadn't encouraged sleeping together. It gave the wrong impression—that he wanted them around apart from for sex.

It must have exhausted Maddi...the walkabout. They were exhausting at the best of times, and today's had gone on an hour longer than scheduled purely because everyone had wanted to see Maddi so much.

No, not Maddi. Princess Laia.

Ari's mouth tightened. He could imagine that if it *had* been Princess Laia there today they would have followed the usual strict sequence of events. The people would have liked her, but that distance would have been there. The distance that anyone growing up as a royal cultivated over time.

She wouldn't have been as open and warm with the people. Holding babies with sticky hands. Hunkering down to talk to children through the barrier. Or to an old lady sitting on a chair. Maddi had spoken to her for long minutes. The woman had been beaming when she'd walked away.

His mother had never even done that. She'd seen a walkabout as something that would dispel the necessary distance they needed to maintain, to perpetuate a vision of the royal family as sacrosanct. Perfect.

It had been anything but. Which was why Ari had always wanted to change things.

He'd changed things already in myriad ways—mainly in the sense of opening things up and presenting a more stable leadership to his people. They'd come to trust that he was different from his mercurial father. He was more dependable. He had the interests of his people at the forefront of everything he did. He was proud of his achievements.

Taking a wife and having a queen by his side was the next step. And, as much as he'd always known it would be Princess Laia, and that she'd do the job well, he had to admit that he hadn't really had a sense of how that might look until today.

Until he'd seen Maddi in action. A woman who was natural and unaffected and warm. Compassionate.

A woman who is not destined to be your Queen.

Had it been a mistake to bring her today? To let the public see her like that? The people had loved her. But, as Maddi had pointed out, they would never see her again.

Ari hadn't really paused to consider the consequences—which was not like him. He'd brought her with him, he realised now, because he'd wanted to see her in action.

As if his gut had already told him what a natural she'd be.

As if his gut was already telling him things he didn't want to consider intellectually.

Things like the fact that he had to acknowledge his marriage with Princess Laia was becoming less and less likely. Not just because of her obvious reluctance and absence, but also because something inside him had shifted.

He'd taken it for granted for so long—when you were told at eight years old that something was destined to happen, it wove its way into the fabric of your life. You didn't question it. But Ari realised now that he'd been arrogantly blinkered about the marriage. He'd merely had it slotted into his schedule like any other meeting or event. He hadn't actually considered the human factor. The possibility that Laia was an autonomous woman who might not want or expect the same thing.

It had taken meeting Maddi to make him see that. And he found, as he considered this now, that it wasn't making him angry or frustrated. If anything, he felt a sense of liberation. As if he'd been carrying a weight for a long time and someone had lifted it from him.

He felt a frisson of excitement. Tantalising possibilities he'd never considered before were opening up. The fact that he could have a queen by his side who he actually liked. Who he liked spending time with. Who he *wanted* with a hunger that grew daily.

But she's not of royal blood.

She was a commoner. Which was why she'd connected so effortlessly with his people. A revelation that Ari didn't like to acknowledge now.

Was he really contemplating a scenario in which a woman like Maddi could be his Queen? It was an impossibility.

No King of Santanger had ever married a commoner. Their family line was one of the most ancient in the world. Academics came to study their family tree because there had never been any dilution of the royal lines on either side. Ari might be intent on bringing Santanger into the modern world, and as much as the people had welcomed the changes, he knew that underneath it all was a love and reverence for their royal family, who epitomised an ancient tradition that had been lost almost everywhere else.

Ari's frisson of excitement was fading. He might not be marrying Princess Laia any more, but Maddi certainly couldn't be a contender. So, no matter what happened, this was still just an affair and he would have to choose a royal bride. Irritating, but not insurmountable.

So why did he suddenly feel burdened again?

Maddi moved minutely on the bed, her eyelashes flickering. Ari welcomed the distraction from those revelations. He took off his jacket and shoes and got onto the bed beside her.

Her eyes opened and focused on him. *Dios*, but she was beautiful.

He traced her jaw with his finger. 'Nice nap?'

She nodded. And then she made a face. 'The truth is I'm starving...for food.'

Being with this woman was not necessarily good for Ari's ego. He laughed.

A little voice whispered at him. *You haven't laughed so much in years.*

He pushed it down. 'I'll order something, shall I?'

Maddi looked almost comically grateful, 'Yes, please.'

When Ari had ordered the food, he felt her arms slide around his waist from behind and his body responded predictably. With a hunger that was as sharp as it had been the first time he'd slept with this woman. A sense of desperation made him feel slightly panicky.

He turned around. Maddi looked up at him.

'Thank you...' she said. 'Maybe before the food comes there's time for a little...appetiser?'

For a second Ari's head told him he had to stop this now. Push her away. Send her back to Isla'Rosa. Princess Laia had made her point. He needed to move on. But Maddi's body against his was a provocation that he couldn't ignore. Or resist.

Feeling reckless and desperate at the inevitable prospect of this ending soon—because it would have to—Ari cupped Maddi's face in his hands. 'I think there might even be time for a little more than an appetiser...'

A few days later

The palace garden party for frontline workers—nurses, police officers, paramedics, fireman, among many others—was a roaring success. There was a bouncy castle for their children in one corner. Face-painting. Clowns. Local vets showing off exotic animals and puppies. Buffet tables were laden with food and refreshments. There would be a fireworks display soon, as the sun set.

It was an annual fixture—something Ari had introduced to open up the palace and say thank you to the people of Santanger. His father had preferred to keep the palace closed off—a place that only the select few got to visit. A place where he could conduct his affairs in private. Hence Ari's decision to do the opposite.

One of his chief aides approached. He said, 'It's going well, Your Majesty. Princess Laia is a breath of fresh air.'

Ari's conscience pricked. More than pricked. He felt guilty. He'd been unexpectedly caught up with business meetings for the past two days, dealing with a minor financial crisis in one of Santanger's banks.

Weakly, he'd used the distraction as an excuse to avoid thinking about what to do about Maddi, when he knew exactly what he had to do. Deal with the fact that Princess Laia was not interested in their strategic marriage and let Maddi go. And yet he was still perpetuating this pretence of an engagement that could never become anything more.

He was playing a very dangerous game.

He tracked her easily in the crowd. She was wearing a teal blue-green dress. Long sleeves, flowing skirt.

Hair coiled up into an elegant chignon. She was talking to a group of nurses and she threw her head back to laugh at something one of them had said. They were all grinning. He couldn't blame them. She was stunning.

After the walkabout she was all anyone could talk about. *Princess Laia this... Princess Laia that...* Exactly as he'd planned it. Except it sat in his gut now with an acrid taste. Because she wasn't Laia. She was Maddi. And he didn't like the fact that his people didn't know who she was.

Which was so messed up—because if they found out who she really was it would invite exactly the kind of scandal Ari wanted to avoid at all costs. It was impossible.

But even now, when he knew all that, all he wanted was to go over, take her by the arm and find somewhere quiet where he could taste her, fill his hands with her firm flesh, make her press against him and moan into his mouth.

But then she disappeared. He couldn't see her any more. He tensed.

His aide said, 'The special effects team are just waiting for your nod to launch the fireworks, Your Majesty.'

Distracted, Ari said, 'Let me find Ma—' He stopped and cursed silently. He was losing it. 'Let me find Princess Laia.'

He moved through the crowd, stopping and starting when people wanted a word, feeling a growing sense of frustration.

Where was she?

He couldn't help but acknowledge the uneasy feeling that if it wasn't for her sense of loyalty to Princess Laia, Maddi might very well just disappear at any moment.

Before he was ready to let her go.

And then he saw her. She was sitting cross-legged on the grass, uncaring of her dress, with a boy of about nine or ten opposite her, also cross-legged. They were locked in an intense discussion.

Ari went closer and saw that a woman was standing nearby. She turned and greeted him, curtseying. 'Your Majesty, I'm so sorry. My son has latched on to Princess Laia and won't hear of letting her go.'

Ari's first rueful thought was, *I know how you feel.*

The woman went on, *sotto voce*, 'He has Asperger's, and doesn't connect easily with people, but she came over to him and just…knew how to talk to him. He's dragged her over here to show her something…'

Ari had always known that having children would be part of his duty as King. But he'd never really thought about what it might feel like. Watching Maddi with this young boy made something tug inside him. He had a sense for the first time that his view of fatherhood had always been too narrow. Not surprising, after the hands-off treatment from his own parents. But he'd never contemplated having something different for himself. For his own family.

The idea rooted in his head, and he realised with a lurch that it wasn't totally ridiculous to want a different, *better* experience. To want more.

And who was the catalyst for yet another unsettling revelation? *Maddi.*

At that moment, as if hearing his thoughts, Maddi looked up and caught his eye.

CHAPTER TEN

WHAT HAD SHE done now? Maddi wondered, the smile slipping off her face. Ari was scowling at her.

Ari had been busy for the past couple of days, and she'd welcomed a little space to try and get her head around this whole situation, which felt as if it was veering way out of control. As if she'd ever had any control over it.

She stood up, feeling defensive and also a little hurt. It seemed that, no matter what, Ari still didn't trust her. She'd found him looking at her warily since the night they'd returned from the walkabout. As if he was trying to figure something out.

She moved to stand in front of him. He was looking at her again with a strange expression.

She said, 'He's a sweet boy.'

Ari's expression cleared. 'You're good with kids.'

'I guess I find it easy to communicate with them.' Maddi shrugged, not liking the little glow she felt at his compliment.

Ari's aide appeared again, and Ari said, 'Give the signal for the fireworks.'

He went back towards the crowd and clapped his

hands, getting everyone's attention. 'Thank you all for coming—please, enjoy the end of the party.'

Maddi followed behind him. Everyone cheered and clapped and then there were *oohs* and *aahs* as the fireworks started, launching high into the sky over the sea before exploding into a million different colours and shapes.

Maddi felt absurdly emotional as she took in the joy of the crowd. Everyone was so lovely here, and they all adored their king. They'd told her that his father had never opened up the palace like this. Or treated them as human beings.

Ari turned and looked at her. He held out his hand and she stepped forward, taking it. Standing by his side when they both knew that this was not real.

'This is a really nice thing to do,' Maddi said, smiling at the joy of the crowd, hoping he wouldn't see her emotion.

She was in deep with this man and there was no way it could end well. She had an awful sense that the end was coming before she was ready for it.

On an impulse, telling herself it wasn't out of a sense of desperation and fear that everything was about to change, Maddi turned to him and said, 'Could we do something this evening? Like…go on a date? Go out for dinner?'

It was ridiculous. Her heart was thumping as if she was a teenager, asking out a boy she fancied. She'd been sleeping with this man for days now, and she knew him more intimately than she knew herself.

Ari put a hand on his chest. 'Are you asking me out on a date?'

Maddi scowled at him and tried to hide her insecurity. He was laughing at her. Reminding her that this was beyond the parameters of...whatever it was between them.

'Forget it—a silly idea.'

She tried to pull her hand out of his but he caught it. She looked up and her insides swooped at the expression on his face. He wasn't mocking any more. There was an intensity there that she hadn't seen before.

'I would love to take you for dinner.'

'I...' She felt tongue-tied. Again, ridiculous, considering how intimate they were. 'Okay...great.'

Ari signalled to his hovering aide, gave him some instructions and then said, 'Let's go.'

But Maddi stopped in her tracks and looked down. She felt self-conscious heat rise in her face. Ari followed her gaze, down to her bare feet.

She looked up, embarrassed. 'Sorry... The last time I saw my sandals a little girl was playing dress-up with them.'

She obviously wasn't ready to be a princess, no matter how much she liked talking to people. But before she knew what was happening Ari bent down and picked Maddi up in his arms and carried her back through the garden and to the palace.

Dammit, but she couldn't help relishing the feeling of being in his arms, cradled against his chest.

She also couldn't stop the soppy grin on her face.

When they got inside the palace there was a sense of infectious energy in the air. Ari put her back on her feet and Hannah appeared and took Maddi by the hand.

She was smiling, and said, 'The things you need are in your room, Princess Laia, come with me.'

Feeling nonplussed, Maddi followed in Hannah's wake as the girl led her up through the endless corridors back to her suite. Once in her rooms, Hannah went to the dressing room and in a few minutes emerged with an armful of clothes.

She laid them out on the bed. Worn jeans, sneakers, a black silk shirt and a beautifully soft cropped black leather jacket. And new underwear.

Maddi went over and touched the leather. 'Ooh, I like this.'

Maddi glanced at Hannah, as if to ask, *Are you sure this is what I have to wear?* and noticed the girl's eyes were shiny.

She immediately went over to her. 'Hannah? Is everything okay?'

She started crying in earnest, and Maddi put her arm around her, leading her into the bathroom. In fits and starts, in between apologies, the girl looked at Maddi with huge blue eyes and said, 'I'm so sorry, Princess Laia, but I'm just so happy to see you and the King like this. My mother worked here too, for the Queen, and she was so unhappy. The atmosphere was always so tense and sad… I'm just so thrilled for you both… and for us. You really love each other, and things will be so different now.'

A solid weight settled in Maddi's belly.

She wiped Hannah's tears and said, 'You're a romantic.'

The girl looked at Maddi and said, so defiantly that Maddi laughed, 'Yes, I am—and I'm not ashamed of it.'

She took Hannah by the shoulders and said, 'Good for you. Don't ever lose it.'

But her conscience mocked her. Who was she to advise someone to keep on believing in romance when she was so busy suppressing her own emotions and deepest fantasies that she had a constant ache in her gut.

What she was doing was making a mockery of Hannah's beautiful, innocent romanticism, but also making a mockery of herself—because she was getting caught up on a flight of fancy too, and the higher it went, the harder the fall would be.

But Hannah was helping her out of her dress now, and into the new clothes. The silk shirt settled around Maddi's shoulders like air. And as she was fastening the buttons, Hannah was undoing her hair and letting it fall down.

She pulled on the jeans and the sneakers. And then Hannah led her back out of the suite and in the opposite direction from the one they usually went. They came out near the palace kitchen garden. In another courtyard.

And there... Maddi's eyes nearly bugged out of her head... Ari was waiting, beside a massive motorbike. Wearing jeans and a T-shirt under a well-loved leather jacket.

She nearly melted on the spot into a pool of lust and longing. He looked so unlike the man who had stepped out of his car that day in the desert in his suit. This man looked wild and young...and so sexy he took her breath away.

He held out a helmet and Maddi walked forward. She didn't know what to say. She hadn't envisaged this at all when she'd told him she wanted to go on a date. She was speechless.

She took the helmet and put it on her head. Then he put on his own helmet and swung his leg over the bike, sitting in the middle.

He held out a hand. 'Use me to balance, stand on the little step and jump on.'

Maddi had never been on a motorbike in her life. She sat on the bike and slid almost naturally into the dip behind Ari.

He said over his shoulder, 'Put your arms around me.'

She needed no encouragement.

Maddi slid her arms around his lean torso and then he straightened the bike. With a downward push of his foot the machine roared to life and throbbed powerfully under Maddi's body.

They left the palace, and Maddi was aware of the ever-present security following them at a distance in a car. They wound their way down the mountain, passing through small villages where people were sitting outside small cafés, children running around.

They approached the outskirts of the city. The tall, gleaming financial district. And then moved into the older part, where the streets buzzed and hummed with activity on this weekend night. It was cool, but still warm enough for people to be outside, strolling around with just a light coat.

Ari pulled up in the middle of a parking area and turned off the bike. Maddi reluctantly disengaged and sat up straight. Ari took off his helmet and she took off hers too, and handed it to him.

'You get off first,' he told her.

She did, and her legs felt wobbly. Then Ari stepped off and stowed their helmets. He handed her a baseball cap and put one on himself. She put it on.

Then he surprised her by taking her hand to lead her out of the quiet square. She stopped and he looked back.

She said, 'I thought we weren't meant to do this.'

He said, 'We're incognito.'

Maddi snorted. 'I might be able to be that, but no one is not going to recognise you.'

'Wait and see—we won't be bothered.'

They emerged onto one of the main streets, busy with evening strollers and people window-shopping the luxurious boutiques. They got a few glances, and Maddi saw some stop and stare, but Ari was right—no one approached.

They wandered up and down the busy streets and Maddi tugged Ari in the direction of the more touristy area. Here there were shops selling stuff for the beach and postcards. She felt a pang. She'd like to send a post-card to her mother, but she couldn't, of course—she had no idea what was going on. She assumed Maddi was in Isla'Rosa.

Then Ari led her down a quiet street from where they emerged into a hidden square. Maddi gasped. The houses were obviously old, some a little higgledy-piggledy. Restaurants lined one side of the square, with tables and chairs spilling outside, and the entirety of the square was strung overhead with fairy lights. There was a low hum of people talking and music. It was magical.

Ari led her over to one restaurant and the owner came out when he saw them. He surprised Maddi by clasping Ari by the shoulders, looking him up and down as if checking he had all his limbs intact, and then kissing him on both cheeks. Maddi had never seen anyone greet Ari so affectionately.

And then Ari was standing back and saying, 'Alfredo, I'd like you to meet Princess Laia.'

It was stinging harder and harder now, every time someone called her Princess Laia. And yet there was nothing Maddi could do about it. She'd put herself in this position and she couldn't afford to reveal her identity until Laia did. But in a way she had to be thankful, because this trip had shown her that she really was ready to embrace her destiny of being a princess. As scared as she still was, the people of Santanger had shown her that she might just be able to do it.

Ari hadn't mentioned the wedding in days now, and she was too cowardly to ask him if he'd finally realised it was not going to happen. Because then he would have no need of her. She couldn't let herself indulge in a fantasy where she told Ari who she really was because it was too seductive. Too dangerous. And her fantasy always played out the same way in the end—it turned into a nightmare. Rejection. Her worst fear.

'Princess Laia, you are so welcome to Santanger and to my humble establishment.'

Alfredo's greeting stopped the spiral in Maddi's head and she welcomed it. He took her hand and charmed her by kissing it. She smiled. He led them into the restaurant, which looked small and cosy from the outside but opened up inside into a beautiful airy space.

The diners were all well-heeled and elegant. Maddi felt distinctly underdressed, and was glad when Alfredo led them to a booth near the back that was secluded but gave them a view of the room.

Ari said, 'The food here is astounding. Alfredo comes from generations of chefs and bakers. His family have continued the tradition and this restaurant is renowned all over the world as offering one of the best Mediterranean menus. His wife is from Turkey and she's brought with her a Middle Eastern fusion.'

Maddi's belly gave a low rumble at that exact moment and she smiled ruefully. 'I could pretend that I'm not that hungry or interested, but what's the point? You know my healthy appetite.'

Ari smiled. 'That's why I know you'll love it here.'

Maddi's heart clenched.

Please don't smile like that.

A waitress approached with two delicate flutes of sparkling wine. She said, 'Compliments of the house.'

Maddi smiled at her, and the waitress blushed and scurried away.

Ari lifted his glass and said, 'This is from a grape native to Santanger—we're busy cultivating our wine industry.'

Maddi took a sip. It was light and dry, with just the right amount of sweetness. 'It's perfect.'

And it was. All so perfect. All so seductive. And the more she enmeshed herself in this reality that was not reality at all, Maddi feared she'd never find her way out.

He might not reject you...just tell him, whispered a rogue little voice.

But Maddi ignored it. It wasn't her truth to tell yet.

Then the food started to arrive, and Maddi let herself be distracted by a selection of starters—including calamari, crisp on the outside and beautifully tender on the inside. There was a selection of mains to share—in particular a tender chicken tagine with couscous and olives and hummus and flat bread...

Maddi was in food heaven.

She glanced at Ari at one point and saw he was just looking at her indulgently, taking a sip of his wine.

She wiped her mouth. 'I'm sorry. I know you're not used to seeing a woman really eat.'

'It's very sexy.'

Maddi's insides liquefied. She took a hurried sip of her own wine to cool down. It was the perfect accompaniment. Crisp and light and fragrant.

'I may never leave this place,' she warned Ari.

'I used to work here.'

Maddi nearly choked on her wine. She put down the glass. 'You what?'

He nodded. 'For a couple of summers when I was a teenager.'

'Was it your father's idea? To try and teach you the ways of humble normal people?'

He scowled at her. 'No, actually. It was my idea. My parents...my mother was becoming unbearable. The tension in the palace was toxic. I came down here one day and asked Alfredo if he'd let me work in the kitchen. I was friends with his son. At first he told me no way, he couldn't be seen to be making the future King work, but I managed to persuade him. I would have been happy washing dishes—anything to get away from the atmosphere in the palace—but he insisted on me working in the kitchen, actually learning something.'

Maddi felt something inside her give way. This was

the exact moment when she knew she was deeply and irrevocably in love with this man…as if up to now she'd been fooling herself into thinking it might not be real. And it filled her with such an acute melancholy that emotion gripped her throat.

It was ironic. Maybe she was destined to be exiled by a king, just as her mother had been.

Somehow she managed to find her voice and not sound as if a storm was tearing her apart inside. 'You never mentioned your culinary skills.'

He made a face. 'It was so long ago now…but it's like learning to type. I can chop anything you want with perfect precision.'

Maddi opened her eyes wide, and brought a hand to her chest. 'You can type too?'

He reached for her and tugged her closer, saying, 'I can type sixty words a minute. But my spelling is atrocious because I'm mildly dyslexic.'

Maddi refused to let the melancholy drag her down. 'Wow, sixty words, and the skill set of a commis chef,' she teased. 'You'll never be unemployable.' And then, more serious, 'You're dyslexic? That must be tough…'

'Both myself and Dax have dyslexia. He's slightly more severe than me.'

'You never mentioned it before.'

Ari shrugged lightly. 'I've learnt to navigate around it. I don't really think of it all that much.'

Maddi lifted a hand to Ari's jaw. 'In a way it's good that you're not completely perfect. You're pretty insufferable as it is.'

He took her hand and pressed a kiss to the palm.

'Oh, I am, am I? I didn't hear you complaining this morning in bed.'

This morning…when he'd woken her by exploring every inch of her flesh and teasing her body into throbbing, aching life. She'd thought she was dreaming, but it hadn't been a dream. But this…*this*, right now, was a dream. A dangerous fantasy she was clinging on to.

They were interrupted by a discreet cough. Maddi blushed and pulled her hand back. Alfredo was looking at them indulgently. Clearly delighted for his King and new Queen-to-be.

The weight in her gut was back.

The waitress deftly cleared their plates and Alfredo deposited new plates in front of them. 'My special baklava, a secret recipe handed down by my wife's relatives.'

Maddi's tastebuds rejoiced. The weight in her gut didn't. It sat there ominously.

Alfredo left and Maddi did her best to hide the fact that she had just realised she loved this man, and everything about Santanger, and yet none of it was hers or had ever been meant to be hers.

She knew the sweetness of the dessert would push her over the edge.

Ari was shocked. 'You're not eating the baklava? I would have bet money that you'd love it.'

Stop it, she begged inwardly. *Stop making me fall even harder for you.*

'I do… But I think I've hit the limit, even for me.' She looked at Ari. 'You have to eat my portion too, because I can't bear for Alfredo to think I didn't like it.'

He looked at her for a long moment with a funny

expression, and then eventually said, 'Okay, but on one condition…'

'What's that?'

'You make it up to me…later.'

In bed. Where they shared the only real thing about this whole situation. Sex.

Maddi hid her growing turmoil behind a smile. 'If you insist.'

When they got back to the palace Ari led Maddi through the dimly lit corridors by the hand, but her mood of melancholy lingered, ominously.

In his rooms, he didn't speak to her. A sense of word-less intensity and urgency filled the air, Maddi tried not to decipher why. Ari pushed her jacket off and to the ground. She kicked off the sneakers. Desperation over-took them as their mouths met and their hands pulled and ripped at clothes until they were both naked and panting.

He led her into the bathroom and reached inside the shower, turning it on. He stepped in, pulling Maddi with him. They were drenched in seconds and surrounded in steam.

Feeling bold, Maddi pressed close and reached up. Twining her arms around Ari's neck and kissing him. Finding his tongue and biting it. His hands rested on her hips, and then he let one drift down between her legs, sliding his fingers between her thighs and mak-ing a sound deep in his throat when he could feel for himself how ready she was.

Maddi was trembling now. She dislodged Ari's hand, because he was going to push her over the edge before she was ready and he did that so easily. She desperately needed to feel some sense of control, and she knew it wasn't just about this moment.

She pressed kisses along his neck and then down further, to his chest...his nipples, biting gently and then soothing him with her tongue, making him clasp her head and pull it back.

'What are you doing?'

She shook her head and continued to kiss her way down his body until she knelt at his feet. A supplicant. But powerful. She took his erection in her hand and heard his indrawn breath.

'Maddi...you don't have to—'

She put her mouth around him, cutting off his words. He tensed. She explored him, tasting every inch of his quivering flesh. She hadn't even realised that he'd turned off the shower. That his hands were curled into fists at his sides to stop himself from stopping her.

It was completely instinctive. This need to pleasure him in a way that would make him crazy. She looked up and almost stopped when she saw the feral look on his face.

When he spoke he was hoarse. 'Maddi, if you don't stop—'

She didn't stop. She kept going until his whole body went still and, with a curse, he lost all control and his hips jerked with his orgasm.

Maddi stood up and Ari opened his eyes. He looked dazed. He was almost slumped back against the glass wall.

'Who are you...?' he said, almost to himself.

He reached out and pushed some of her hair back

over her shoulder. For a crazy moment Maddi felt like
Delilah with Samson, but Ari's strength soon returned.
He stood up and turned the water back on. He turned
Maddi so she was facing the glass. Their reflections
looked back at her.

'Put up your hands.'

She did so, her whole body tingling with anticipation. First, Ari soaped her whole body, with particular
attention to between her legs. Maddi was squirming,
but Ari held her hips fast. He stepped up behind her.
She could feel his total recovery and wanted to curse
his virility. Of course he wasn't going to let her have
her moment of control.

He cupped her breasts and trapped her nipples between his fingers. She spread her fingers wide on the
glass, back arching, pressing into him. She could feel
him taking himself in his hand and pressing the head
of his erection against her slick body, sliding between
her legs.

'Bend down a little,' he instructed.

Maddi did, and Ari thrust into her in one smooth,
cataclysmic movement. He bent over her and squeezed
her breasts as he moved in and out. Water and steam
enveloped them. Maddi was half crazed, pushing back
against Ari, silently begging for *more...harder.*

It was fast and furious. Maddi's body clenched tight
and then exploded into an ocean of pleasure. Ari extricated himself from Maddi's embrace and she let out a
little sound as her sensitised muscles released him. She
was barely aware of him taking his own release safely,
under the powerful spray of water. Once again showing that he had more presence of mind than she did.

Ari bundled her into a towel and dried her. Then he carried her to the bed and she passed out in a haze of lingering pleasure and satisfaction.

She woke at some point later to find herself cocooned in Ari's embrace, her bottom snugly against his growing erection and his hand on her breast.

She moved against him and silently, only stopping for him to put on protection, they made love again as furiously as before…as if they were being driven by all the silent voices around them whispering that this couldn't possibly last…

CHAPTER ELEVEN

MADDI WOKE FEELING DISORIENTATED. The bed was empty, but only the faintest trails of dawn lightened the sky outside. She lay there for a moment, orientating herself. There had been an edge to their lovemaking last night. An edge that hadn't been there before... As if they'd both been aware that time was running out and...

Maddi didn't even want to think about it.

But you have to. This is getting ridiculous. Unsupportable.

She sat up, pulling the sheet around her. A chill breeze skated over her skin even though there was no window or door open. She got out of the bed and pulled on a robe, went looking for Ari.

Had she heard a phone ringing a while ago? Had she heard Ari's voice, low and deep? Was that what had woken her? Maybe she'd been dreaming.

He was in his informal living room, standing watching a news channel.

She was momentarily distracted by the fact that he was only wearing sweatpants, his broad back bare.

For some reason he looked remote. Untouchable. Maddi came closer and saw what he was looking at on the screen. Her insides fell to the floor. She might have fallen to the floor too, if she hadn't locked her knees.

On the screen was footage of Princess Laia, arriving back into Isla'Rosa on the royal jet. She looked both glowing and drawn at the same time. Tense. It was the first time Maddi had laid eyes on her in… How long had it been? It felt like aeons. But it had just been weeks.

Reporters were calling out to her as she emerged from the plane. 'Princess Laia, what about your engagement to King Aristedes? Why did you leave Santanger?'

Maddi realised with a jolt that they obviously believed Laia had flown in from Santanger. And why wouldn't they? She'd been here for the last few weeks with her fiancé, as far as the world was aware.

Except she hadn't been. Maddi had. Living in a make-believe land that was now collapsing around her.

Her brain hurt as she tried to untangle what this all meant.

At that moment Princess Laia looked at the camera and said, very clearly, 'I have no comment to make at this time except to say that I'm looking forward to my coronation in a few days' time.'

Laia's birthday.

Maddi realised that they had done it. Laia had managed to get back to Isla'Rosa just in time for her birthday and her coronation.

At that moment Ari flicked a switch and the TV went black. There was a heavy silence in the room. He knew she was there.

Without turning around, he said, 'As you can see, your job here is done.'

Maddi went cold inside at the detached tone of his

voice. She walked to stand in front of him. He looked impossibly remote. Like a stranger. Not like the man who had made love to her just short hours before with such hunger.

'Ari…'

He looked at her and she almost took a step back. His face and eyes were devoid of all expression.

'I'll arrange for Hannah to come and help you pack your things. You'll leave the country discreetly, to minimise the chances of anyone seeing you.'

It took a second for what he meant to sink in. *Of course.* If anyone saw her here, then it would expose both him and Princess Laia. Obviously she had to go.

'And then what?'

'And then what, Maddi? Then you get on with your life as Princess Laia's—sorry, as *Queen* Laia's lady-in-waiting. What did you think?'

What had she thought?

She'd known this was coming. She'd felt it last night. And for the last few days. Like a sword hanging over her head. In a way it was almost a relief. She wouldn't have to pretend to be someone else any more.

It was a relief tempered with such pain, though.

As if she had to hear him say it to be sure, she said, 'This is it then…? Even once Laia has become Queen you don't…we can't see each other again?'

Maddi had wanted to make it sound like a statement, but it came out like a question.

He smiled, but it was mirthless. 'No, Maddi. I told you not to confuse sex with emotion. You said you knew what you were getting into. But maybe the great sex confused you. Because it was amazing sex. I'll grant you that. For a novice you were…spectacular.'

For a second Maddi was so outraged she couldn't speak. She'd never hit another person in her life, but right now she wanted to strike at Ari and his hateful words.

She'd been such a fool to allow intimacy to grow between them. Her anger started to burn, and she welcomed it because it was cauterising her raw wound.

'Don't patronise me, Ari. I might have been physically innocent, but I'm not emotionally naive. And thank you for the compliment. You've certainly opened my eyes as to what to expect from a satisfying lover. I won't settle for less in future.'

His jaw clenched at that, but it was small comfort.

He said, 'Be honest, Maddi, what were you really hoping for? A declaration of love?'

Pain lanced Maddi's heart. *Yes.*

'No, not that. I know what you think of love. That it's an indulgence that leads only to weakness and self-destruction. But not everyone is your mother, Ari. Some people learn to get over their heartache and find another kind of love. My mother didn't let it destroy her.'

Like his had done.

'None of that interests me. It's time for you to go back where you belong.'

I belong here, with you.

The words rose up on a tide of emotion that Maddi did her best to hold back. He was right—she did need to go back to Laia and reorientate herself. It was clear she was no longer welcome here. She never really had been. Ari had spied an opportunity to have some fun while she was here, and he'd taken it.

So did you.

Suddenly Maddi didn't have the stomach for hiding behind bravado.

'You didn't have to be tender, Ari. You could have spared me that. But then I guess this was always going to be an exercise in punishment for you, wasn't it? After all, you didn't get your convenient queen.'

'I'm not so petty. The first night we slept together was the start of my letting go of the marriage agreement with Princess Laia. Did you really think I could have a situation in which I was married to a woman while my ex-lover worked as her lady-in-waiting?'

Maddi didn't know what to say.

Ari went on. Grim. 'I realised then that this whole agreement with Laia was something I'd taken for granted. Hadn't really thought about. Certainly I hadn't considered her feelings. She tried to speak to me years ago, after her father's funeral. I know that I barely entertained her concerns. I told her it was happening and that was that. I'm not proud to admit that.'

Maddi swallowed the emotion in her throat. 'What about the peace agreement?'

He looked at her. Still cold as ice. 'That'll be between me and Queen Laia, but I have no doubt we can work something out.'

'So, all's well that ends well?'

Maddi knew she should be happy for her sister that Ari had come to this realisation of his own arrogance and stubbornness, and was showing a willingness not to let their actions affect the peace agreement. But she felt hollow.

And she must be a sucker for punishment, because she said, 'I'm sorry for the inconvenience. You'll have to find a new royal bride, but I'm sure you will.'

Ari said nothing—just looked at her. Silently telling her to leave.

Maddi turned and walked to the door. She'd been right to fear the pain of this rejection. It was like a knife lodged in her gut. Sharp and devastating.

She had felt as if she had a place here—but not any more. She was unwelcome. Unwanted. The magic that she'd thought existed between her and Ari had all been an illusion. He was right. She'd confused sex with emotion, just as he'd said.

She was almost at the door when Ari said from behind her, 'You're obviously not applying for the position yourself?'

Maddi stopped dead. Had she misheard him?

She turned around. 'What did you say?'

'You heard me,' he all but spat out.

He knows.

His remote demeanour now made sense.

Maddi felt unbelievably cold. Exposed. 'How did you know?'

When did he know? Has he known all along?

Questions buzzed in her head, causing a cacophony.

'I asked a friend to have you investigated when I realised you weren't Princess Laia.'

Maddi might have objected to that if she'd had any right to. But she'd given up that right when she'd lied about who she was.

'When did you know?'

'Only a few hours ago. Your secret was a well-kept one, *Princess Maddi*.'

Maddi winced. 'It's not like that. I always knew, but my father…the King…made my mother agree that she wouldn't make any claim to the royal family on my behalf as long as he was alive and paying her maintenance. When he died…she was ill. I wasn't interested in finding out more. Thankfully she recovered but she never mentioned it and neither did I.'

Ari was facing her now, arms folded across his chest, muscles bulging. Even now distracting. His expression was almost sneering.

'If I didn't know you I'd assume you were lying. Who on earth would pass up the chance of entering a life of unparalleled privilege and luxury? No one but you.'

Maddi was sure he didn't mean that as a compliment.

Then he said, 'Maybe it's time you faced up to the responsibility you bear, Maddi Smith. Time to step out of the shadows and stop playing at being someone else.'

Maddi whispered, 'That's not fair.'

She'd only just finally begun to believe that she could.

'Isn't it?'

His words resonated deep inside. Why hadn't she wanted to pursue her birthright after her father had died? She could have gone to Laia long before Laia had come looking for her. She'd told herself she hadn't been interested, as if she had some higher loftier ideal than wanting a life of luxury, but perhaps the reason was more prosaic than that.

A fear of rejection. Rejection by her sister. And by

the people of Isla'Rosa. She'd never fully acknowledged this before now.

Fear had stopped her. Selfish fear of being hurt. She wasn't brave and selfless, like Laia and Ari. She didn't deserve to be a princess—even though these past couple of weeks had given her a real sense that she *could* be. And that she wanted to be.

Somehow she managed to make her voice sound strong. As if she wasn't falling apart inside. 'Goodbye, Ari. I'm sorry…for everything.'

She left before she could hear if he'd even said goodbye. Probably not.

Everything happened so quickly after that. Her head was spinning by the time she was being ushered onto a small sleek jet as the sky lightened in the east…heralding another beautiful day in Santanger.

First of all, she'd deceived King Aristedes. Then she'd deceived the people of Santanger. But worst of all, she'd deceived herself.

Ari watched the small plane take off into the brightening sky. Just like that she was gone. The woman who had come into his life and turned it upside down and inside out. With her bare feet and her gap-toothed grin and her insatiable appetite—*appetites*.

His blood heated and he cursed out loud and turned away from the sight of the plane.

Damn her.

Damn her.

The marriage agreement with Princess Laia and Isla'Rosa was obviously dead in the water. But Ari had come to terms with that. There would be some other way around uniting their two countries in a peace agreement, although the marriage would have been a much neater way of doing it.

As much as he didn't want to credit her with anything, he had to admit that Maddi had been the catalyst in helping him to see how entrenched he'd been about the idea of marriage. He had to concede that if Princess Laia had come to him again, to try and talk to him, he might very well not have heard her—*again*. He would have done everything in his power to persuade her.

And perhaps that was what she'd been afraid of— that he would try to appeal to the side of her that feared for Isla'Rosa's future, the side of her that had grown up with a strongly ingrained sense of duty and responsibility. As had he.

Ari went over to his drinks cabinet. It wasn't even nine a.m. but he didn't care as he threw a shot of whisky down his throat.

Maddi had deceived him. She'd come here with one agenda—to protect her Queen. *No*, her sister. Her half-sister.

He still couldn't quite believe what Antonio Chatsfield had told him. His friend had said, 'You might want to sit down for this, my friend.'

Her father was the late King of Isla'Rosa. He was the man who had abandoned her mother.

Ari considered that for a moment—how she must have felt growing up, knowing that she was a princess but being forced into exile. And not becoming bitter about that. It would take an extraordinary human not to be swayed by such temptation.

And then to work as the Queen's lady-in-waiting for

a year. Why had she done that? Why hadn't she wanted the world to know she was part of the royal family?

He couldn't ask her now, because she was gone.

Maddening, infuriating woman.

Her words came back to him. *'You didn't have to be tender.'*

No, there had been no need for tenderness. But with her he hadn't been in control of his impulses.

Passion didn't last, he told himself now—desperately. It never had in the past. It had burned bright, or not even that bright, and then faded like a dying firework. *This*, however—this thing that was between them—wasn't fading. Not even now that he knew the full extent of her betrayal.

But she hadn't told him the full truth of who she was, and that stung more than anything.

He'd trusted her. In spite of her initial deception. And he'd only realised the profundity of how easily that had happened when his friend had told him who she really was. Yet she hadn't trusted him.

He'd been harsh. He'd never been harsh with a woman before. Because no other woman had ever got under his skin before. And not just under his skin. Into his gut. Into his head.

Into his emotions.

He'd learnt from his parents that uncontrollable desire and love were self-destructive. He'd lived his life believing that he was immune to those things. His life was all about control. And that included his emotions. Until now.

It burned him to admit this, but he'd actually imagined her by his side. He'd imagined somehow being able to bring her in front of his people and have them accept her, even though he'd believed she wasn't of royal blood.

Because he hadn't been able to countenance the thought of not having her by his side...in his bed. And yet she hadn't trusted him with vital information. Proof that he was the fool. The idiot who had forgotten the lessons of a lifetime...

He slugged back another shot of whisky and cursed Maddi Smith again. He would ban her from Santanger. He would find a suitable royal princess and get on with the task at hand. Being King and siring heirs.

And all these rogue thoughts of perhaps being an actual father and wanting something different for the first time in his life, wanting *more*, would be pushed back down where they belonged.

There was a sound at the door and Ari turned around, his heart leaping, making a total mockery of his recent thoughts. But it wasn't her. It was someone else.

His brother.

He looked at Dax across the room and was filled with such a sense of incoherent rage for everything that had happened that he said, 'Where the hell have you been?'

Dax looked as grim as Ari felt. He also looked a little wild. Jaw heavily stubbled and hair too long. His brother was wearing faded jeans and a wrinkled shirt. He looked as disreputable as he always did. But there was something different about him that Ari couldn't put his finger on, but it resonated in him as if he recognised what it was instinctively.

A woman.

His brother came in and arched a brow. 'Drinking before noon, Ari? Have you decided to join my gang?'

Dax smiled, but it was mirthless as he helped himself to a shot of whisky, quickly downed it and then filled his glass with another.

Ari looked at him. 'Dax…?'

Dax looked at him. 'I'm sorry, Ari.'

'For what?'

'For not bringing Laia back in time. We were… She has this island in Malaysia. That's where we've been. I couldn't leave.'

Then a look that Ari couldn't decipher came over Dax's face. There was something fierce about it.

'You know you can't marry her, right?'

Ari said, 'Yes, I know.'

The ferocity left Dax's face. He said, 'You'll find another princess.'

Ari might have smiled at the notion that princesses could just be found—if he'd felt remotely inclined to smile. But right now he was done with princesses.

'What happened between you and Princess Laia?' he asked.

Dax avoided his eye. Guilty.

Ari said wearily, 'It's not as if I can't put two and two together, Dax. I had no hold over her. It was an ancient agreement. I barely knew her.'

Dax looked at him. 'I tried not to…but…' he trailed off.

Ari could almost sympathise. They'd both been tied in knots by the Isla'Rosa Princesses.

He asked, 'Did you know Laia was Maddi's half-sister?'

Dax nodded and sat down on a chair, long legs sprawled out. 'But I couldn't get in touch with you. She threw my phone into the sea…'

Ari thought back to Maddi, throwing her phone out the window, and barked out a sudden laugh.

Dax leant forward. 'What's so funny? This is a disaster.'

Ari sobered. Dax was right. It wasn't funny at all. And suddenly there was a weight such as he'd never felt before, settling in his gut and spreading up into his chest, tightening like a vice.

'Maddi!'

Laia flew across her office and all but jumped into Maddi's arms.

Maddi hugged her tight. Anything to avoid the awful emotion that threatened to spill over at any moment.

Laia pulled back and ran her hands all over Maddi, as if checking for broken bones. 'Are you okay? Did he let you leave today or did you have to escape? I can't believe he kept you there and made you pretend to be me—'

Maddi couldn't let her go on. 'Laia, it wasn't like that. He found out almost straight away that I wasn't you. But no one else knew. I agreed to slot into your engagement schedule because I thought that was the best way of letting you stay hidden. But the truth is...'

She moved out of Laia's embrace and went to the window to try and collect herself.

'Mads?'

She turned around. 'The truth is that I fell for him. We...we were together.'

Laia paled. 'Oh... Oh, wow. I didn't expect that... but I guess it was pretty apparent.'

Maddi frowned. 'What do you mean?'

Laia took her hand and led her over to the desk, where a laptop was open. Laia had clearly been looking at pictures of Maddi and Ari on their public engagements. There was the walkabout, and Ari leading her away with an indulgent smile as Maddi waved at the crowd, a huge grin on her face. And someone had taken a snap of him carrying her away from the garden party for frontline workers into the palace.

She blushed.

Laia said, 'I thought he was going to keep you on Santanger as some sort of a threat. That he wouldn't release you unless I agreed to the marriage. But he let you go…'

A knife sank into Maddi's heart. 'Yes, he let me go.' She had to give him his due. 'Laia, he knows your marriage is off the table. He realised a while ago that he'd done you a disservice in just assuming you'd marry him. He told me that you'd tried to talk to him years ago and that he all but ignored you.'

'Oh, well…that's good. Did he say anything about the peace agreement?'

Maddi nodded. 'That he's sure you can discuss it at some point.'

Laia's eyes widened. 'Wow! Maybe I didn't give him enough credit.'

'He never really forced me to stay there, Laia. I… I wanted to be there, as strange as it sounds.' She looked at Laia sheepishly. 'I enjoyed it…pretending to be you… as scary as it was. But it was starting to take a toll… not being me.'

Laia smiled wryly. 'I can imagine.'

Maddi took her hands. 'But Ari doesn't want me, and

none of that matters. What matters is that you're back
in time for your coronation and there's nothing and no
one to stop you becoming Queen.'

A shadow passed across Laia's face and Maddi was
immediately concerned. 'What is it? What are you not
telling me? Did Ari's brother Dax find you? Did something happen?'

Laia went pale and shook her head. 'It's okay. I'll
tell you about it later.'

As if wanting to divert Maddi from any more questions, Laia said, 'I'll draft a statement, saying that by
mutual agreement King Aristedes and I have decided
not to proceed with our marriage. I'll send it over to
him to see if he'll accept that.'

Maddi smiled, but it felt wobbly. 'I'm sure he will.
He's a good man, Laia. I think you'll like him when
you do have talks.'

Laia saw her emotion and touched Maddi's cheek.
'Oh, Mads, I'm sorry…is there any hope?'

Maddi shook her head fiercely and hoped she
wouldn't start crying. 'No, he made that clear from
the start. And at the end. It wasn't as if I didn't know.'

But that hadn't stopped her hoping.

Laia said, 'Well, you're back where you belong. And
I want everyone to know who you are…if you're ready?'

Maddi thought of Ari saying, *'Maybe it's time to step
out of the shadows…'*

She smiled and took a deep breath. 'Yes, I'm ready.'

Laia gave a whoop, and hugged Maddi again, and
Maddi tried her best to focus on the present and the
new future that would unfold for her. A new future in
which she would try and forget the man who had awo-

ken her to a dazzling new version of herself only to crush it to pieces.

She hated Aristedes.

She hated him as much as she loved him.

CHAPTER TWELVE

Two weeks later

ARI SWITCHED OFF THE TV. He'd watched Maddi being crowned Princess of Isla'Rosa on a loop since Laia's coronation over a week ago.

He'd agreed to the statement put out by Princess Laia about the demise of their engagement, and she'd had the grace to phone him and apologise for all the theatrics. They'd arranged a future date to talk about how to proceed with building peace between their countries.

He'd had to bite his lip to stop himself asking about Maddi.

He wanted nothing to do with her. He never wanted to see her again.

Except every night in his dreams, when he couldn't stop her from intruding. They veered from being X-rated, when he would wake with a raging, burning desire that only a cold shower could cure, to dreams where she was running away from him, laughing, disappearing down corridors or into rooms that were empty when he burst inside.

He was losing it. He was so grumpy that Dax had left

to go back to New York, where he was mainly based. Come to think of it, Dax hadn't exactly been in good form either.

Ari had found him watching a rerun of the coronation of Queen Laia with an intensity that had made Ari ask, 'Is there anything else you'd like to share about what happened on that island with Laia, Dax?'

For the first time since they were kids Ari had thought Dax might actually hit him. His brother had snarled at him to mind his own business and stormed out of the room.

It was late. Ari had meetings in the morning. He should sleep. But he knew he'd only have those dreams again.

Damn her.

He sat down at his desk. There was a light knock at the door. Probably Santo, wondering if he needed anything.

Ari called out without looking up. 'Come in.'

The door opened and then shut again quickly. Santo didn't speak. Ari looked up, and at first he wasn't sure who he was looking at. Someone all in black, wearing a baseball cap.

Then whoever it was tipped up their face. A rush of blood to Ari's head was his first reaction. And then a wave of heat to every cell in his body.

'How dare you come back here?'

He stood up and put his hands on the table. Was he, in fact, dreaming?

She moved forward and took off the hat. Her hair spilled down around her shoulders. She was wearing a black sweatshirt and black sweatpants. Black shoes.

Her voice was husky. 'I'm sorry... I needed to see you.'

'How did you get in here?'

'I... I contacted someone. It doesn't matter who. They helped me.'

Ari still wasn't entirely sure he wasn't dreaming.

'Come closer. I need to be sure it's you and not Queen Laia. Perhaps you're not done playing your games.'

Maddi stepped forward. She looked pale. 'It's me.'

It was her. He wasn't dreaming.

There was such a mix of volatile emotions raging in his gut that he had to take a second to try and contain them. He'd never had to deal with emotions before.

Damn her again.

He said, 'To what do I owe the pleasure of a midnight visit from the newly crowned Princess Maddi of Isla'Rosa?'

Maddi tried not to quiver under the scathing tone and icy glare of Ari. She'd known this would be difficult, but she wouldn't be able to move on completely until she'd faced her last fears and told him how she felt. She refused to let fear rule her life again.

She swallowed. 'I came here because I want to tell you something.'

Ari put out a hand. 'Please, be my guest. Would you like a drink? Perhaps some of that whisky?'

Maddi felt a flicker of anger at Ari's bullish mood.

She lifted her chin. 'Actually, yes, that would be lovely—if it's not too much trouble.'

'Oh, it's no trouble at all.'

He went into the living area and Maddi followed him, drinking him in. He was wearing jeans and a shirt, sleeves rolled up, top button open. There was stubble on his jaw and his hair was mussed, as if he'd been running a hand through it. When he turned around to hand her the glass she noticed that he looked a little drawn.

Her heart hitched.

Because of her?

Was he having crazy dreams too?

She downed the shot and handed back the glass. 'Another, please.' She needed all the courage she could muster.

He looked at her for a long moment, but then took the glass and refilled it, handing it back. She downed this one too, and put the glass on the table. Her head was spinning momentarily, and heat flooded her upper chest.

He folded his arms. 'So, you wanted to tell me something?'

Maddi wondered if she had gone totally mad. She was literally inviting him to inflict even more pain on her than he had done already. But if she didn't do this… she'd regret it for ever.

She said clearly, 'Yes. I came here to tell you that I love you, Aristedes. When you asked me if I was looking for a declaration of love and I said no, I was too scared to admit it, but actually I was.'

She held up a hand, even though he hadn't opened his mouth to speak.

'And do *not* patronise me by telling me I fell for you because you were my first lover and all that nonsense. This is a once-in-a-lifetime love that transcends sex. I think you have feelings for me and that's why you're so angry,' she went on. 'Because you didn't want any of this either. And because I didn't tell you who I really was. I need to explain why...'

'Go on.'

Ari was grim. Not exactly encouraging, but Maddi couldn't go back now.

She shrugged minutely. 'In a nutshell, because you're right. I was hiding in the shadows. I could have come to find Laia after our father died, to claim my birthright, but I didn't. I told myself I wasn't interested in becoming a princess or living in that world. But the truth is that I was terrified of risking rejection. So I waited until she came to me. When my father sent my mother into exile it was before I was even born. He rejected me before he even knew me. That...that put a mark on me for my whole life. And I never realised how deep it went until you made me see it.'

She ploughed on.

'And then, when I came here...met you... I told myself that I couldn't betray Laia's confidence. She wanted to reveal my identity when the time was right for her. I couldn't risk you using the information to wreak some kind of revenge...or that's what I told myself. But really I was still tied to the fear of rejection. I fantasised about telling you who I was...but I was terrified you'd still reject me. So it was fear—again.'

Ari said nothing. Maddi couldn't read his expression. She was too scared to.

'I came here tonight to tell you how I feel because if there's any chance that you might feel the same way then I would like to have a life with you, Ari. Loving you and getting to know every part of you. For ever. But if you don't then at least you'll know how I feel. I know having a life with you would also mean my becoming Queen, and I'm barely used to being a princess…but I would try my best to do you proud. Because I love you. So much.'

Maddi stood there for a long moment. Emotionally naked and exposed.

Ari was looking at her with wide eyes. She didn't know if it was a look of shock, or disgust, or—

She realised as the silence wore on that she didn't want to know. Clearly he didn't know how to respond because he didn't feel an atom of what she felt.

Devastation quietly settled in her gut, cold and frigid. She took a step back. Still he didn't do anything or say anything.

'Okay, look… Please don't use this as an opportunity to mock me, Ari. Just let me leave with a little dignity. You won't ever see me again. I promise.'

Somehow Maddi was able to make her legs move and she took one step in front of another and went towards the door.

Just as she put her hand on the knob she felt movement behind her, and the door was kept shut by Ari's hands on it, over her head. He was caging her in.

He said, 'You are going nowhere. You are never leaving this palace again.'

Maddi placed her forehead against the door. 'Ari, I'm sorry for what happened, okay? And the fact that the marriage didn't happen—'

Ari put his hands on Maddi's shoulders and spun her around so fast her head was spinning again.

'Ari…?' She looked up at him, and the expression on his face dissolved any words she might have said.

It was crazed. His eyes were burning.

'I am so over that marriage not happening,' he said. 'I'm not letting you leave here because if you do I won't be able to live. I've only been half living since you left.'

'Since you let me leave,' she said shakily.

He shook his head. 'I was so angry. You came into my life like a whirlwind and upended everything I knew. My nice, neat, complacent life. You stirred up every emotion I've ever had and hidden, and some new ones that I don't think have even been invented yet.'

Maddi hardly dared to breathe. 'Is that a good thing?'

Ari barked out a laugh. 'I think it's only a good thing if you're here to help me regulate them.'

'You want me to stay?'

'Yes, please.'

'Like...as your...guest...? Before you marry someone suitable?'

Ari glared at her. 'Don't you get it yet? It's you, Maddi. Only you. There will be no one else. I'm so fathoms deep in love with you that I'm drowning, and you're the only one who can save me.'

Maddi's heart cracked open. 'Why did you let me go? Why didn't you come for me?'

'Because I'm an idiot and a coward and I was hurt that you hadn't trusted me.'

Maddi bit her lip. 'I'm so sorry... I did trust you. I just didn't trust myself.' They looked at each other for a long moment, and then Maddi said, 'What if I hadn't come today?'

'Then I probably would have stayed miserable and angry for another week, or maybe even a month, but eventually I would have realised I was losing the best thing that ever happened to me. *You.*'

Maddi jumped into Ari's arms, wrapping hers around his neck, taking him by surprise and propelling him backwards. They lost balance and fell back onto the floor. They landed with an *oof.*

Maddi was plastered to Ari's front. She lifted her head. 'I'm sorry, are you okay?'

Ari winced. 'My back might be broken, but I don't care.'

He demonstrated that he was fine by shifting them so that she was on her back under him and he was over her. She twined her arms around his neck again.

'Do you really mean it? Are you sure you're not confusing emotion with sex?'

He smirked. 'Don't patronise me, Maddi. This is a once-in-a-lifetime love. I might not have asked for it, but I'm here for it.'

'Me too.' She smiled tremulously and reached up, pressing her mouth to Ari's. He kissed her back, hard and passionate, snaking his arm under her back to arch her into his chest. She spread her legs so that he fell into the cradle of her hips, and she could feel his body responding to hers.

He stopped the kiss and Maddi opened blurry eyes. Ari was taking something out of his pocket. The engagement ring. She'd left it behind.

He said, 'I've been carrying this around since you left it behind. Taking it out…looking at it…cursing you for making me into someone I didn't recognise.' He shook his head. 'And I've been having dreams—'

'Me too!' said Maddi. 'Crazy dreams, where I can't find you.'

Ari looked down at her, and his face was filled

with something that made Maddi's heart sing. Emotion and *love.*

He took her hand and put the ring back on her finger. 'Well, now we've found each other again,' he said. 'I don't want to ever lose you, Maddi. I would die.'

'Me too. I love you, Ari.'

He kissed her palm and then pulled her up to sit, and then stand. He got down on one knee in front of her, still holding her hand. Maddi's hair was dishevelled, and she wore no make-up, and she was dressed in athleisure wear. But she couldn't care less.

'Maddi Smith... *Princess Maddi*...would you please do me the honour of becoming my wife and Queen of Santanger?'

A tiny sliver of fear made her shiver. She hated herself for it, but she had to ask... 'What if I can't do it, Ari? I hardly know how to be a princess... I don't want to let you down.'

Ari stood up and cupped her face in his hands. 'You will be the perfect queen for me and for Santanger. You proved that within just two weeks. The people love you. I love you. You can do anything you want. This is your destiny, and I want everyone to see *you* and know how amazing you are.'

Maddi melted all over. 'Thank you,' she whispered. 'That's the nicest thing anyone has ever said to me.'

He got down on one knee again. 'Now, can you please answer the question? Will you marry me?'

Maddi nodded, her eyes swimming with tears. 'Yes, please. I'd like that a lot.'

Ari stood up and cupped her face in his hands and kissed her, long and slow and thorough. Then he picked

her up and carried her through the palace to his rooms—
their rooms—and showed her exactly how much he
loved her with his body and his whispered words.

As dawn broke outside, many hours later, they were
both awake, still revelling in the amazingness of being
together and in love. Pledging their lives to each other
for ever.

Maddi tilted her head back and looked at Ari. 'What
if I hadn't been related to Princess Laia…? What if I'd
just been a regular person?'

Ari came up on one elbow and looked at her. He
smiled. 'I'd already instructed my staff to look up the
constitution and see how it might be possible for me
to marry you.'

Maddi sat up. 'You had? When?'

Ari pulled her back down to his chest. 'The day of
the garden party.'

'Oh, my…'

Maddi's heart swelled in her chest. Any lingering
doubts or fears were well and truly gone.

'Oh, my, indeed,' Ari echoed.

After a moment, Maddi asked, 'Do you think we
could have a press conference?'

'For what?'

'I want to apologise to the people of Santanger for
misleading them about who I was…'

'That's my apology to make. It was my choice.'

Maddi shook her head. 'It was me too. I didn't have
to agree. I could have left. But I love them, and I don't
want them to think I disrespected them.'

Ari looked at her. 'You're amazing—you know that?'

Maddi shrugged, shy.

Ari said, 'We'll do a press conference to announce our engagement and wedding. And you can say what you have to say.'

A week later, they did the press conference. Maddi was nervous, but she spoke from the heart.

And then Ari took her hand and said to the people of Santanger, 'This is the woman you fell in love with... who I fell in love with. She will be my wife and your Queen.'

There was a moment of silence as the press pack and the crowd absorbed what they'd said, and then there was a spontaneous outbreak of applause and cheering. Maddi saw suspiciously bright eyes in the most hardened of hacks.

A month later, Maddi and Ari emerged into bright, early spring sunshine outside the cathedral of Santanger. She was a vision in a long white dress—simple and classic, overlaid with Santanger lace—with a long veil and a glittering tiara.

She turned to Ari and, grinning, forgot every bit of protocol she'd been taught about how to behave in public. She threw her arms around his neck and pressed her mouth to his.

He mentally threw out the protocol book too, and wrapped his arms around his wife...his *Queen*...and kissed her back with all the passion that raged between them, while the crowd cheered and clapped and cried and threw flowers in the air.

Their marriage signalled a new era for the royal family of Santanger and a lasting peace with Isla'Rosa.

A couple of days later Maddi and Ari were in their honeymoon villa, high in the mountains, with epic views over the island. Maddi had insisted on having a honeymoon on the island, wanting to share her happiness with the people as much as possible.

The sun was setting outside, and everything was bathed in a golden glow.

They'd made love and were basking in a post-coital haze of satisfaction. And not a little emotion. When Ari had reached for protection just a short while before, Maddi had stopped him. Silently they'd communicated the step they were taking, and she was mortified to admit now that she'd cried a little at the thought of creating a family and doing it with love.

She hoped that, for them, it would be different. It would. She knew it, deep in her bones.

She turned her face to Ari and kissed his chest. 'I love you...'

He squeezed her bare buttock.

She smiled.

He said, 'I love you, Queen Maddi of Santanger.'

Through the haze of happiness and satisfaction something occurred to her and she lifted her head.

'Have you heard from Dax?'

Ari shook his head. 'No—should I have?'

Maddi frowned. 'No... I guess not. It's just that I haven't heard from Laia either. She left after the wedding reception. She said something about an emergency she had to get home for, but that it wasn't too serious. I'm pretty sure I saw Dax leaving not long afterwards.'

Ari pulled Maddi down onto his chest, crushing her

breasts against him. Maddi's brain immediately became fuzzy.

He said, 'Something happened between them on that island, but he's never said what.'

'Neither has Laia.'

Maddi might have thought about how she'd felt a little hurt by that, but she was becoming distracted by her husband's roving hands.

Ari said, 'They're both grown-ups. I'm sure they're fine and they'll figure it out.'

Maddi slid over Ari's body and spread her legs either side of his hips. Every inch of them was touching. Ari's eyes flashed dark and golden.

She said, 'You mean like we did?'

Ari smiled wickedly as he smoothed a hand over Maddi's buttock again, before squeezing hard. She sucked in a breath.

He said, 'Exactly. Just like we did.'

Maddi grinned. 'Then they'll need all the help they can get.'

Ari slapped her lightly, mock-outraged. 'What are you insinuating?'

Maddi kissed him. 'Nothing—except for the fact that I'm so glad we did figure it out.'

Ari flipped them easily, so he was on top, between Maddi's legs. She luxuriated in his solid weight and wrapped her legs around his waist, inviting him into a more intimate embrace. He didn't need any encouragement.

That day was a good day.

And so was every day after that.

The people of Santanger loved their Queen Maddi

as much as the King did. Well, maybe not *as* much.
That would have been impossible. Because theirs was
a once-in-a-lifetime love and they proved it, by living
a long and happy life, in love and in passion, every day.

* * * * *

If you couldn't put
Mistaken as His Royal Bride *down,*
be sure to check out the next instalment in the
Princess Brides for Royal Brothers *duet,*
coming next month!

In the meantime, get lost in these other
Abby Green stories!

Bound by Her Shocking Secret
Their One-Night Rio Reunion
The Kiss She Claimed from the Greek
A Ring for the Spaniard's Revenge
His Housekeeper's Twin Baby Confession

Available now!

COMING NEXT MONTH FROM

HARLEQUIN

PRESENTS

#4161 BOUND BY HER BABY REVELATION
Hot Winter Escapes
by Cathy Williams

Kaya's late mentor was like a second mother to her. So Kaya's astounded to learn she won't inherit her home—her mentor's secret son will. Tycoon Leo plans to sell the property and return to his world. But soon their impalpable desire leaves them forever bound by the consequence...

#4162 AN HEIR MADE IN HAWAII
Hot Winter Escapes
by Emmy Grayson

Nicholas Lassard never planned to be a father. But when business negotiations with Anika Pierce lead to his penthouse, she's left with bombshell news. He vows to give his child the upbringing he never had, but before that, he must admit that their connection runs far deeper than their passion...

#4163 CLAIMED BY THE CROWN PRINCE
Hot Winter Escapes
by Abby Green

Fleeing an arranged marriage to a king is easy for Princess Laia—remaining hidden is harder! When his brother, Crown Prince Dax, tracks her down, he strands them on a private island. Laia's unprepared for their chemistry, and ten days alone in paradise makes it impossible to avoid temptation!

#4164 ONE FORBIDDEN NIGHT IN PARADISE
Hot Winter Escapes
by Louise Fuller

House-sitting an idyllic beachside villa gives Jemima Friday the solitude she craves after a gut-wrenching betrayal. So when she runs into charismatic stranger Chase, their instant heat is a complication she doesn't need! Until they share a night of unrivaled pleasure on his lavish yacht, and it changes *everything*...

HPCNMRA1123

#4165 A NINE-MONTH DEAL WITH HER HUSBAND
Hot Winter Escapes
by Joss Wood
Millie Piper's on-paper marriage to CEO Benedikt Jónsson gave her ownership over her life and her billion-dollar inheritance. Now Millie wants a baby, so it's only right that she asks Ben for a divorce first. She doesn't expect her shocking attraction to her convenient husband! Dare she propose that *Ben* father her child?

#4166 SNOWBOUND WITH THE IRRESISTIBLE SICILIAN
Hot Winter Escapes
by Maya Blake
Shy Giada Parker can't believe she agreed to take her überconfident twin's place in securing work with ruthless Alessio Montaldi. Until a blizzard strands her in Alessio's opulent Swiss chalet and steeling her body against his magnetic gaze becomes Giada's hardest challenge yet!

#4167 UNDOING HIS INNOCENT ENEMY
Hot Winter Escapes
by Heidi Rice
Wildlife photographer Cara prizes her independence as the only way to avoid risky emotional entanglements. Until a storm traps her in reclusive billionaire Logan's luxurious lodge, and there's nowhere to hide from their sexual tension! Logan's everything Cara shouldn't want but he's all she craves...

#4168 IN BED WITH HER BILLIONAIRE BODYGUARD
Hot Winter Escapes
by Pippa Roscoe
Visiting an Austrian ski resort is the first step in Hope Harcourt's plan to take back her family's luxury empire. Having the gorgeous security magnate Luca Calvino follow her every move, protecting her from her unscrupulous rivals, isn't! Especially when their forbidden relationship begins to cross a line...

YOU CAN FIND MORE INFORMATION ON UPCOMING HARLEQUIN TITLES, FREE EXCERPTS AND MORE AT HARLEQUIN.COM.

HPCNMRB1123

HARLEQUIN
PLUS

Try the best multimedia subscription service for romance readers like you!

Read, Watch and Play.

Experience the easiest way to get the romance content you crave.

Start your **FREE TRIAL** at
<u>www.harlequinplus.com/freetrial</u>.